FLIRTATIOUS

K.M. SCOTT

BOOKS BY K.M. SCOTT

Crash Into Me (Heart of Stone #1)

Fall Into Me (Heart of Stone #2)

Give In To Me (Heart of Stone #3)

Heart of Stone Volume One

Ever After (Heart of Stone #4)

A Heart of Stone Christmas (Heart of Stone #5)

Return To Me (Heart of Stone #6)

Forever With Me (Heart of Stone #7)

Heart of Stone Volume Two

Hard As Stone (Heart of Stone #8)

Set In Stone (Heart of Stone #9)

Silent As A Stone (Heart of Stone #10)

Heart of Stone Volume Three

All of Me (Heart of Stone #11)

Temptation (Club X #1)

Surrender (Club X #2)

Possession (Club X #3)

Satisfaction (Club X #4)

Acceptance (Club X #5)

Notorious (NeXt #1)

BOOKS BY K.M. SCOTT WRITING AS GABRIELLE BISSET

Blood Avenged (Sons of Navarus #1)

Blood Betrayed (Sons of Navarus #2)

Blood Spirit (Sons of Navarus #3)

Blood Prophecy (Sons of Navarus #4)

Blood Craving (Sons of Navarus #5)

Blood Eclipse (Sons of Navarus #6)

Blood Ascendant (Sons of Navarus #7)

Stolen Destiny (Destined Ones Duology #1)

Destiny Redeemed (Destined Ones Duology #2)

Love's Master

Masquerade

The Victorian Erotic Romance Trilogy

FLIRTATIOUS

From *New York Times* bestselling author K.M. Scott comes a sexy opposites attract romance about two people who couldn't be more different yet couldn't be more right for one another.

Liam Jackson personifies the old saying, "Still waters run deep." He keeps to himself, and he'd probably be a hermit living in a cave in the woods if it weren't for his large family.

As the son of Kane Jackson, he's a lot like his father.

Mia Shanoff lives in the spotlight. The newest star in the music business, she's so big the mere mention of her makes the media go wild. Her story is one everyone wants to know more about.

But you know what they say. Don't believe everything you hear.

For Liam, the madness of Mia's world makes his job protecting her harder than he'd like. Mia's new bodyguard is far too sexy for her not to notice him, yet he's far too by the book.

Can two people so completely opposite ever have a chance together?

CHAPTER ONE

ia

How many talking heads are going to get in on giving their opinion about my life? Their unneeded and unsolicited opinion, as far as I'm concerned.

You'd think these people would have better things to do than dissect every misstep and bad relationship I've had in the past few years. I mean, there is an entire world out there revolving around all sorts of things like war and famine and a million other terrible realities, yet these clowns yammer on and on about Mia this and Mia that.

I stretch my legs out across the king size hotel bed with the divine blue comforter and sheets to die for and feel the tension dissipate as I mute the TV. These sheets are heavenly. White cotton like any other I've slept in, but oh my God are they comfortable. I'm guessing they have to be at least twelve hundred thread count. I need to find out who makes them so I can get a set for my own bed back at the house.

The house. Ugh. Where everyone, no doubt, is rushing to and fro while pulling their hair out by the roots as they fret needlessly about where I might be. For a moment, I close my eyes and picture everyone looking in horror at their hands full of hair. Just something else to stress out about. It would be amusing if it wasn't so ridiculous.

I can hear all their worrying from here. The queen of worry, my mother, is the worst. "She could be dead in a ditch on the side of the road," she wails like some fool, all the while wringing her hands.

I've never even seen a ditch, much less been in one, dead or alive.

"Maybe someone kidnapped her?" Chloe and Ivy suggest in unison like they often do when they're excited about something.

Why my makeup artists are always so melodramatic is beyond me. Nobody kidnapped me. They know that and still I'm betting they've already said those exact words, which of course, made everyone else freak out even more.

I take a deep breath and let it out slowly, allowing my shoulders to come back down from around my ears. Maybe they wouldn't be totally off the mark with their concern. I've had more than one stalker since I got big, but none of those guys were ever the kidnapper type. They're more the kind of people who yearn from afar, but if they ever did get close enough to touch me, they'd probably piss their pants.

My life coach Ainsley is probably attempting, with little luck, to calm everyone down with her Zen sayings none of them will listen to. I like when she does her quiet pep talks, but then again, I'm willing to pay attention and consider the ideas she's presenting.

My mother and my entourage aren't fans of the Zen stuff, though. They prefer to swirl around in madness and chaos, which is the reason I had to hire Ainsley as my life coach in the first place.

I glance over at the TV sitting in the dark cherry wood cabinet across the hotel room and see some gray-haired news guy still talking about my sudden disappearance, but now they have an image of my ex Jonny positioned next to the old guy's head. What on earth could they be saying about my ex-boyfriend?

Unmuting the TV, I heard gray hair explain who Jonny is. Only an old dude like you wouldn't know he's the lead singer of the band Punk Slut, man. Jesus. Get with the times already. If you don't know what the hell you're discussing, maybe you should stick to segments on shitty politics or the climate crisis you don't really give a shit about and leave the current stuff to cooler people.

"I'm here with Doctor Elizabeth Walters, a psychologist on staff at New York's Mercy Hospital whose research on the interpersonal and sexual dynamics of the stars focuses on exactly the kind of issues Mia's had with her romantic relationships," old news guy says in his oh-so-solemn tone.

Holy shit! Are they really going to dive into my relationship with Jonny because I've been out of the public's sight for forty-eight hours? Here's a hint, Doc. We're going to need more time than they've given you to hash out that mess. Jonny and I were a toxic trainwreck from our first kiss.

Do they really think I went back to him? Don't they pay attention to the gossip that says he's with that chick who's the lead singer for Banshee? Guess which couple is fighting tonight, for sure.

"Doctor Walters, if a young woman like Mia were to go missing, as she has, what is the likelihood she'd fall back into old, destructive patterns and return to an ex-boyfriend, even one as notoriously abusive as Jonny Chambers was with Mia?"

Fuck, there's a lot to unpack there. I don't think the pretty lady with the perfectly coiffed brunette bob is going to be able to tackle all of that. She was hoping to use this time to pimp her new self-help book she just knows is exactly what women need in this crazy world.

As I suspected before she began talking, Doctor Walters struggles to say anything definitive. Probably because she's never spoken a single goddamned word to me nor I her. Nice of them to try to diagnose me from miles away.

Not satisfied to assume the worst about me back with my shitty ex-boyfriend, old news guy introduces his second guest, another renowned shrink from some big city hospital I don't catch before he asks him, "Doctor Chesterbrook, as a psychologist trained to see destructive patterns in patients when it comes to addiction, what can you tell me about all you know concerning Mia?"

Curious how they plan to connect my recent stint in rehab with wanting to disappear from the limelight for two damn days, I sit up and listen to the African American doctor with the giant glasses.

"Well, Mason, I have never been one of Mia's doctors, but I'm seeing patterns I don't like with this young woman's life. I just hope her friends and family are seeing them too and doing all they can to get her the help she needs."

Damn, Chesterbrook, the doctor with the name that sounds like every rehab I've ever heard of. You were going so well there when you actually admitted you've never been within three feet of me, so you don't know a damn thing about me, but then you fell back into what I suspect is your usual spiel about patterns and my needing help.

Two fucking days is all I wanted. Two days without anyone talking to me or telling me what I should do or what I shouldn't do. Two damn days of peace and quiet in a great hotel room with junk food nobody ever thinks I should eat and a bathtub where I can soak in a bubble bath until my fingertips and toes get all pruney.

Is that so much to ask?

As I glance across the room at the third doctor Mason Cooperman has added to his collection of quacks all eager to talk about my problems, I know the answer is yes. Forty-eight hours, the last two of which I've spent watching these fools, and the entire world acts like it's been set on fire.

Trust me, people. You'd want a couple days alone too if you were me.

I gather up all the wonderful hotel pillows and make a wall next to the headboard as I laugh at all their guesses about me, what I'm doing, and what could be wrong to make me run away like they suspect I have. The lady doctor with the perfect brown hair is absolutely sure I'm off somewhere having a horrible time with my ex but thinking I'm in love. Chesterbrook with the googly glasses is terribly concerned I've fallen off the wagon and I'm drinking again and possibly back to using coke, which troubles him even more.

Dude, you have no idea. Honestly, you are so off base I can't even find you on the map.

And the third doctor, whose name I don't know because I'm no longer interested in giving them names, thinks that his book, Why Good Women Love Bad Boys, contains the answer to all my problems. I can't focus much on what he's saying because his forehead is so big, it's distracting. Damn, man, we could show movies on that space.

Wow. If I didn't laugh right now, I'd cry at how clueless these assholes are.

My tour that lasted eight months took me to five of

the seven continents and hundreds of cities around the world. I've broken up with one guy, sworn off men entirely, and tragically, I'm rumored to have turned to booze and drugs. The reason why they don't give a damn about, but my being lonely after performances that left me feeling like a wrung-out dishrag might be a good place for everyone to start. I'm tired and my body aches after all those shows, and I'm only nineteen years old, but damnit, these jackasses and everyone else in the world is absolutely sure I'm off doing something destructive.

No mention about how hard I push myself to give audiences the best show they could ever experience. No hint about what it's like to be a homeless singer, living out of suitcases and missing your bed night after night. Not a peep about what it's like to feel like you're living in a fishbowl and every damn supposed journalist has their nose pressed to the glass, dying to catch me doing something that will get them a big scoop. Not a word about the fact that I'm still getting my bearings in life and it's not the end of the world if I make a mistake or two.

Or ten.

No, that would be boring. Instead, they diagnose from afar and make claims they can't possibly back up because they don't know me. They know the public face I put on, but they don't know me. They see Mia, the superstar, not Mia the person.

For four years, I've tried to be everything the world wants me to be. Can't I take forty-eight hours to be just who I want to be for once?

Mason with the gray hair interrupts the female doctor to say my mother is about to come out to hold a press conference. Good to know she isn't letting a chance go by to make this an even bigger circus. I'd hate to think she could just sit tight for a couple days and let me be alone.

I watch as Andrea Shanoff stands in front of the bank of microphones looking entirely too upset for the circumstances. My mother's a beautiful woman with long dark hair that lays perfectly against her head like Cher's did when she was young back in the day. I wish my hair would do that, but with every time my stylists insist on doing something interesting with my look for the crowds who come to see me, the chance that my hair will ever simply hang normally again becomes less and less likely.

Today, she's gone for a light brown jacket over a tan blouse, a look meant to convey her utter despair over my being missing. It's all very earthy and grounded, making me think she took some cues from Ainsley when she was getting ready for this performance of hers. She's gone with less makeup than she usually prefers too. No fake lashes or heavy eyeliner to accent her dark brown eyes. She wants to let the world know that this whole thing has been so trying for her.

"Thank you for all your concern about Mia. I'm here today to make another plea for whoever has her to let her come home. My daughter is a beautiful person, inside and out. She loves to share her God-given gift of her beautiful voice, and I only ask that you release her so all of us can hear her sing again."

I hear the words come out with the right emotion attached to each syllable, but the whole thing sounds hollow to my ears. All I see is panic that her control over me is slipping away. She looked much like this right after I turned eighteen and went off with Jonny to his place in Miami. That press conference was one for the ages. She should have won an Oscar for all that crying and wringing of her hands that her baby was dead in a ditch somewhere.

It's always a ditch with the drama queens.

She likes to fall back on the tried and true ideas. I imagine she'll mention that at some point in this press conference too, but I turn off the TV before she gets the opportunity. Something about her fascination with me in a ditch on the side of the road unnerves me.

I'm my mother's meal ticket. Sure, she loves me, but what she loves more is the lifestyle she has because of my fame and success. At fifteen, I had my first number one song. That was followed by two more before the record company and my manager, my mother, decided that I needed to get my ass out on tour since that's where the big money is.

So tour I did.

I celebrated my sixteenth birthday alone in the back of my tour bus right outside of Tucson. Everyone else had fallen asleep after congratulating me on that night's show, and I sat with a cupcake that Michael, one of my bodyguards, had left me. Carrot cake with cream cheese frosting, my favorite. My version of a sweet sixteen party.

It's thanks to him that I have this hotel room to lounge around in for a couple days. Thank God there's someone I can rely on to understand I need to decompress sometimes.

My seventeenth birthday I celebrated on stage in Rio de Janeiro with thousands of my closest friends waving banners with my name on them while I sang my version of Happy Birthday. They loved it. All I wanted was someone to sing it to me.

That never happened that night. Instead, we all boarded a plane to Mexico City and by the time we landed, the day had ended and I didn't even get a cupcake.

By the time I turned eighteen, I was the biggest star in the world. And the loneliest. I had an entourage around me at all times, especially once the crazy letters from stalkers began to come and my mother felt the need to hire more people.

But eighteen was different because then I was officially an adult. I could be who I wanted to be. I could do what I wanted to do. I could theoretically say no to doing what I didn't want to do because I was an adult.

So, when Jonny Chambers with all his tattoos and piercings came to meet me after one of my shows a few weeks after I turned eighteen, I went back to his hotel room with him and lost my virginity. In retrospect, he wasn't my best choice to lose my V card, but I can't change the past.

As a belated eighteenth birthday present, he took me away to his place in Miami and gave me the biggest party the world has ever seen. The tabloids are still writing about it to this day over a year later. It's the reason why all the talking heads and shrinks on TV are so sure I'm with him right now.

They never saw what happened behind the scenes with us. They think they know things because he was all into drinking and coke when I was with him, and I had bruises they were sure were from him hitting me.

That wasn't what happened, though. He never hit me. What he did was worse. He made me feel like I was just another girl in his harem, that I didn't mean anything to him and he could replace me as easily as he found me.

Since I broke up with him, everyone's talked about how I was abused, and I guess in a lot of ways I was. Jonny never physically abused me, but he did a number on my confidence, so that's a kind of abuse, I think.

That's all behind me now, though. I've got someone I care about in my life who cares about me enough to risk God only knows what my mother might do if she ever finds out Michael was the one who got me this room. He protects me from what really can hurt me, and that means more than I can ever tell him.

To hell with everyone but Michael. My mother, every damn person who thinks they know my life better than I do, and all these jackasses on TV who spend their days and nights talking endlessly about things they know nothing about.

Sliding off the bed, I walk toward the bathroom with the oversized bathtub, the main reason I wanted to come to this hotel. It was a risk since it's the best hotel in the Tampa area, but once I saw the picture of the bathtubs in their suites, I knew this was the place I wanted to hide out and simply relax for a few days.

I turn on the hot water full blast and drop a lavender bubble bomb in to create the perfect luxurious bath experience. As I undress out of my favorite pink yoga pants and white T-shirt that says Superstar in silver across the chest, I catch a glimpse of myself in the enormous bathroom mirror. Two days of gorging on junk food hasn't done nearly as much damage as my personal trainer claimed it would.

For a moment, I pose and smile at the thought of what Mitchell would do if he saw how much I ate in the past forty-eight hours. The guy would have a total meltdown and order me to work out twice as hard for the next month.

"See? I knew a couple days being bad wouldn't do that much damage," I say with a laugh as I climb into the tub.

The water stings it's so hot, so I quickly turn on the cold water to balance things out so I don't give myself second degree burns from the waist down. I pull the cooler water back toward me, which eases the temperature a little, before leaning back against the edge of the tub and closing my eyes.

This is all I wanted when I ran away. Not to fall off the supposed wagon, unless you count candy, cookies, potato chips, and diet soda falling off the wagon. Not to hurt anyone. Just to relax in a tub full of bubbles that smell like flowers after eating too much food that's bad for me for a couple days.

Meanwhile, the entire world outside this hotel suite is spinning out of control worried about what I'm doing. That's their problem, not mine. Maybe they should try some of Ainsley's Zen shit. Maybe then they'd calm the hell down.

CHAPTER TWO

iam

THE LATE APRIL SUN FEELS GOOD ON MY SKIN, SO I push off heading inside to take a few more minutes out here on my balcony. Glancing back toward the glass doors, I see Wilder pacing back and forth through my living room. Every day it's something more stressful with him. If our parents only knew how much trouble he brought into his life simply by being Wilder.

Then again, I doubt my father would be able to see that if it was written on a billboard and he was forced to stand in front of it for hours. Something about my younger brother makes Kane Jackson believe in things that simply don't exist.

I try not to agree with Cade and Alex about Wilder, but he makes it hard. Damn hard sometimes.

Today's crisis involves someone he's been seeing.

For as much trouble as he gets into, he always seems to find room in his life for romance. You'd think they'd see him and all the nonsense he brings with him coming from a mile away, but he flashes them that Wilder smile and they get a look at his tats and piercings, and before you can say "You should have run by now," he's got himself a brand-new love in his life.

He tried to talk to me about whatever this new one's doing last night, but I got the hell out of that conversation before it turned into an hour long discussion of whether or not he should drop all the other ones. It seems this one thinks it should only be the two of them in this relationship. My younger brother has never defined exclusive exactly that way.

As all of this rambles through my brain, threatening to ruin a beautiful day I was hoping to have all to myself, I hear the sliding glass door open behind me and know I should have run like his new love interest. Crashing into my quiet enjoyment of this sunny morning, Wilder sits himself down on the chair across from me and shakes his head.

As if he's got such a tough life that I should feel bad for him.

"It looks like I'm going to have to stay a little while longer. Hope you're okay with that."

I let out a heavy sigh. I don't really have much of a choice. He's family. Yes, he's an asshole and yes, he's an imposition, but my mother pulled me aside last month and begged me to let my brother stay here for a while so she and my father could enjoy some peace and quiet together. Since I thought I'd be on a job somewhere already, I happily agreed.

And then that job fell through when the client's husband realized his wife was the one sending herself threatening notes just to get attention and she didn't need security guarding her against herself. That left me here with my least favorite houseguest in the world.

Who now has just announced he's going to have to stay here a little while longer. To other people, that might mean a day or so. To Wilder Jackson, that could mean months.

Or even longer.

I cringe at the idea of the two of us being permanent roommates. If only his new addition to the harem wasn't so insistent on being the only one in his life.

"Explain to me again why you can't go hang out with one of the multitude of people who've paraded through here in the past few weeks?"

Wilder gets a faraway look in his eyes, like I've asked him some deep question that makes him rethink everything he's ever thought about love. Or parades. You can never tell with him. He's a weird combination of a dreamer and a criminal, so his thoughts go off in tangents I don't even try to understand anymore.

"They're nothing to me," he says in a tone that sounds like he's making some grand pronouncement. "Chris is the one. I know it."

I know what I say next won't register with him the way it would with other people, but I say it anyway because someone has to inject some logic into our lives here. "Then break it off with all the others. This isn't rocket science, man. If this one's the one, then go balls to the wall with this relationship and forget the others."

And just like that, his grand pronouncement look like he's posing for a statue fades away and he sags back in the chair. "I know this is the one. I'm sure of it. I just don't know if I want to give up everything I have going with everyone else yet. You know how it is."

In truth, I don't. I can't fathom running my life the way he does. Or more correctly, the way he's been allowed to since he came into our family. Nothing ever seems permanent to Wilder, despite the fact that he claims he's found the perfect soulmate or the perfect job or even the perfect club to go to practically every week.

That's not who I am. He's all over the place, scattered with everything from his thoughts to his feelings. I'm the opposite. I like my life calm and stable. The last thing I need is unnecessary drama, something my younger brother seems to crave.

There's no point in discussing that with him, though. He thinks his life is perfectly grand. That he causes upheaval everywhere he goes doesn't seem to faze him in the least.

"What about your friends, those guys you hang out with? You can't stay with one of them?"

He dismisses that out of hand with a shake of his head. "They all have lives to lead and girlfriends who live with them now. It's like in the past year every single one of them has gotten tied down," he answers with a healthy dose of disgust for his friends' happily ever afters.

This Chris should definitely run. Now.

"You, on the other hand, are a single guy with two bedrooms, so I figured you'd like the company," he adds.

I guess I should be thankful Wilder has saved me from a life of peace and tranquility. If I could get him to stay still long enough, maybe he could pose for a statue in his honor.

A hundred things pop into my head that I want to say about what he figured I'd like, but I remember my mother and her big blue eyes looking up at me as she pleaded for some time alone with my father and without Wilder. So I simply shrug and stuff all those ideas into a place in the back of my mind for some other time.

"Well, I tend to keep to myself, but feel free to stay as long as you like," I say before closing my eyes.

If he walks back into the apartment right now, this morning won't be totally ruined.

Wilder slaps me on the arm, and my eyes fly open to see him standing next to me looking far too excited. "Great! You know, Liam, we're brothers, so we should hang out more. I know we're as different as night and day, but we've got more in common than you think."

I look up at him as not a single thing comes to me that we may have in common. We're brothers because our parents adopted him, so we don't even share blood, even though he oddly looks like me with his dark hair and blue eyes. Other than looking like we're related, I can't think of a single thing we like that's the same. Or anything that we dislike together either.

"Stay as long as you need to, Wilder. Mi casa es su casa."

"Terrific! I'm thirsty. You want anything to drink?" he asks.

I shake my head as one thing in common between us occurs to me. We both came into the same amount of money when we turned twenty-one. Wilder pissed away nearly every dime of his on partying, sex, and then restitution to pay back for his crime that got him sent to jail. I, on the other hand, have all that I got and more after some wise investments.

He slams the glass door harder than it needs to be shut, and I shake my head again. We have nothing in common.

I get maybe another ten minutes of peace in the sun before my phone rings. Grabbing it off the table next to where I sit, I hold it in front of me as my eyes adjust to see my cell's screen. VIP Security. Maybe there's a job for me after all.

Before I can even say hello, a man's voice begins speaking. "Liam, this is Jonah Bradley, president of VIP Security. I know we haven't spoken many times in the past, but I wanted to be the one to call you with a new assignment because you're the perfect man for the job."

Sitting up, I try to remember any time Jonah Bradley and I have spoken in the past. Maybe once at the Christmas party VIP held two years ago? No, that was his assistant I was talking to near that punchbowl of eggnog that ended up nearly leveling him after someone dumped what must have been an entire bottle of rum into it.

"Hello, Mr. Bradley. I appreciate you thinking of me for this job you believe I'm perfect for. It's nice to be recognized for my hard work."

"Fantastic! You've heard of Mia, the young singer whose name is on everyone's lips? She needs a security chief, and you're the right man for the job."

He sounds like an Army recruiting ad, except working as Mia's head of security would be a hell of a lot worse than enlisting in the military. Last year, she ran away and ended up in rehab after her people finally wrangled her somewhere in south Florida. Then when she got out, she insisted she didn't need a new bodyguard, which meant I'd waited all that time while she dried out for nothing.

No way I wanted to be saddled with this assignment. Nope. No thanks.

"This is the classical pianist I was supposed to go protect who ended up in rehab?" I ask, wanting to make sure I've got the right crazy person in mind.

Jonah hesitates for a moment before answering, "Yeah, well, about that whole pianist thing…forget everything you thought you knew about her because today's a new day."

Now he sounds like someone recruiting people to join a cult.

"I appreciate being in consideration, but I think this time I'm going to have to pass, Mr. Bradley. We tried this last year. It didn't work. I think someone else would be more appropriate."

Still, he doesn't give up.

"Nonsense. You're the best man I have, Liam. You might not know that I actually pay attention to the company I run, but I do and I've seen what clients say about you. You're professional and get the job done. No muss, no fuss. That's exactly the kind of attitude necessary for this assignment."

I replay all the news coverage I've seen in the past few days about Mia being missing and the shitshow surrounding it. No man in his right mind would want to step into that mess. That girl and her life are nothing but a hassle.

"It all seems pretty moot anyway, doesn't it?" I ask, knowing if he's calling me that something's changed with her situation. "She's been missing for forty-eight hours. Seems to me this is like closing the barn door after the horses have all left the barn."

"I'm happy you've been keeping up. That's good news! As for Mia being missing, that's been mostly a show for the press. Andrea Shanoff, Mia's mother, never misses an opportunity to create a media spectacle. They found out her previous head of security got her a room at some hotel with the help of his sister a day ago. Andrea's just been milking the madness."

What part of that is supposed to make me want to take this job? First, her drug and alcohol binge landed her in rehab, and then she balked at getting a new bodyguard at all once she got out. At least now I know it had nothing to do specifically with me. Mia simply didn't want to exchange an indulgent babysitter for an actual security professional intent on taking care of business.

But being the guy who has to deal with replacing the one who got her the room sounds like a thankless job. She's probably way too close to him and is going to kick and scream if her people try to fire him.

On top of all of that, she sounds like a huge pain in the ass. I've got enough money that I don't have to work. I choose to because sitting around day after day gets boring. Also, I want to make my own way in the world, even if I do have a nest egg to fall back on. If it means I have to dip into my money instead of going to work for the world's biggest diva, I vote for raiding the piggy bank.

"I think I'll pass. I'm not great with out-of-control children."

"Liam, I really need you on this assignment," Bradley says in a very different voice from just a minute ago. Now he sounds almost desperate.

My morning relaxation ruined, I stand from the chaise lounge and head back inside. "I wish I could, but this just doesn't sound like the kind of job I want to take. I'm sorry, Mr. Bradley, but Mia's just too much hassle. I hope you find someone. I do."

"I understand. Thanks for hearing me out, Liam."

As I stuff the phone back into my jeans pocket, I wonder if that's the last time I'll be hearing from VIP Security. If it is, so be it. Some hills you just have to die on.

Hiding out from having to spend any more time with Wilder, I try to find a spot down near the water where no one can see me. Since it's one of the usual Jackson-March family get-togethers, that's unlikely, but a guy can try.

I get approximately sixty seconds of alone time before Alex finds me. Slapping me on the back, he laughs as he hands me a beer. "Trying to be invisible, Liam? Who are you avoiding?"

When I shrug and roll my eyes, he answers for me. "Let me guess. That brother of yours. Dude, I heard your father talking at the restaurant the other day. Is he seriously living with you now? That sucks big time for you, I'm sure."

As much as I don't want to talk shit about Wilder, I need to vent to someone, and since Alex probably won't go telling anyone but Cade, I don't censor myself. "You have no fucking idea. The guy is ubiquitous. I swear there are clones of him in every room of my place. I know it's not very brotherly of me, but I think I might end up chucking him off the balcony if he doesn't find somewhere else to go and soon."

Alex sits down on the sand and raises his bottle to tap it off the neck of mine. "To family. They drive you crazy, but what can you do?"

I take a gulp of beer and mumble, "Toss him off the fifth floor of my building."

"You know, I thought I heard my father say

something about him bringing someone with him today, but I didn't see anyone new. Just the typical couples of Cade and Hailey and Cash and Savannah, along with our parents and Stefan and Shay. That leaves Grandma and the rest of us single guys in the family."

Again, I roll my eyes. "The current love of his life probably figured out it's time to run for the hills before it gets really serious. That's why he says he needs to stay at my place for a little longer. 'This is the one,' he says, but he doesn't want to give up all the others."

With a hearty laugh, Alex shakes his head. "Then this one's not the one."

"That's what I told him. He doesn't listen. Then again, has he ever?" I ask, knowing the answer without my cousin giving his opinion.

From the porch, my mother calls out, "Liam! Alex! Come up and join us. Wilder was just talking about how much fun he's having staying with you, honey."

Nudging his elbow into my side, Alex jokes, "Yeah, honey. Let's go talk to your mother about how much fun you're having living with Wilder."

As we reluctantly give up our hiding place, I say to Alex, "Fuckin A. I should have taken that job, except for the fact that it would have been exchanging one pain in the ass for another."

"Which one is that? You still waiting for that girl to get her shit in gear? Isn't she the one who's been missing for forty-eight hours? Have they found her yet?" he asks with genuine concern in his voice.

I shake my head as what Jonah Bradley told me

about that whole missing stunt she pulled this week. While we walk up the stairs to the back porch of my grandmother's house, I explain, "Yeah, she's fine. Well, she's not harmed. The whole thing sounds like it was a publicity stunt to me."

Turning to look at me, Alex seems surprised. "Oh, yeah? So she was never really missing?"

Before I can answer, my mother asks, "Who was missing?"

I really didn't want to have this conversation today since I'm trying to forget Mia and her circus of madness. Waving away my mother's question, I say, "No one. So what's going on up here?"

Cassian and my father sit off to the side talking about something in hushed tones. That means they're either trying to discuss business, which isn't supposed to be allowed at these family events, or they're planning something for Olivia or my mother. Shay and Stefan sit on the other side of the porch talking with my grandmother, leaving the middle of the porch to my mother and Olivia since Cash and Cade and their girlfriends seem to have disappeared, along with Wilder.

"Your father and your uncle are breaking the rules again, aren't they?" my grandmother says loudly. "Cassian and Kane, if you aren't planning some surprise party for one of your wives, you better get over here and join the rest of us. This is supposed to be a party. No talking about the restaurant allowed."

As they look over with guilty expressions and reluctantly move their chairs to the middle of the porch, my mother presses me for a second time about the missing person I was talking to Alex about on our way up here. "So who was missing? Are they okay?"

I open my mouth to deflect attention to my missing cousins and their girlfriends, but just as I begin to say their names, the two happy couples walk out the back door to join us all. Hoping to take advantage of that, I smile and say, "Just these four. Long time, no see. Where have you guys been?"

Cade senses I'm trying to push attention onto them and gives me a knowing smile. "In the house getting something to drink. So who was missing?"

I level a glare at him and shake my head. "Payback's going to be a bitch, dude."

Cash decides to join in and ask the same question, and within a few seconds, everyone on the goddamned porch is asking about who's missing. Jesus, this family is like a dog with a bone once they get onto a topic.

Since it's obvious I'm going to have to answer their question if this party is ever going to even have a chance of getting better, I say, "Mia. The singer. Well, I thought she was a pianist, but that seems to have been some mistake. She was missing. Now she's not. Are all you amateur sleuths satisfied? Now how about we turn the conversation to something interesting, like if today's the day we find out one of the happy couples are getting married."

Unfortunately, nobody takes the bait. From the other side of the porch, my grandmother chuckles. "He's just like you, Kane. We're not going to fall for whatever subterfuge this is, Liam. Everyone knows you're working for that girl, so what's the scoop?"

So much for moving on. Once Alexandria March decides we're talking about something, we're damn well talking about that and only that. Fucking terrific.

"I'm not working for her. That fell through months ago. She's crazy on wheels, so when they asked me again to take on being her security chief, I politely declined."

Cash slaps me on the shoulder and laughs. "That's not your circus and those aren't your monkeys? Sounds like you made the right move considering all I've been seeing on TV about her. That press conference with her mother made it sound like some terrorists had taken her. So she's okay?"

"She's fine, so we can all stop talking about it since it has nothing to do with me or any of us. Time for a new subject. How about the one where the happy couples tell us all when the big days are?" I suggest before taking another gulp of beer.

I'm going to need a whole lot more of that if this party doesn't stop being a discussion of Mia and her insanity. The only thing worse would be everyone asking how living with Wilder is going.

Since my mother can't leave well enough alone, she asks, "Why did you turn down that assignment? I thought you were a lock for that."

As much as I want to say every reason I have can be found in the hour after hour of news coverage of Mia and her disappearance over the past few days, I simply smile and answer, "It didn't feel right, Mom. I'm not the right kind of person for that job."

Everyone around us agrees, but my mother won't let the subject die. "I disagree, honey. You're exactly what that girl needs and desperately, I might add. I've watched all the news reports about her. She needs someone to set her on the right path, Liam."

Looking down into her blue eyes so full of earnest concern for someone she's never met, I can't help but think my mother's too kind for this world. "Mom, she's never going to change. Too many years of being allowed to run wild means she would never want to work with anyone like me. For God's sake, her last chief of security was the person who helped her run away. It's not my job to set someone on the right path."

I want to add that if I could do that, I'd try it with her other son, but I don't. If I think this topic is tiresome, that's nothing compared to the Wilder discussion. Most of the family thinks he's good for nothing, but my parents keep hoping against hope that he'll turn out to be that sweet, wonderful person they're so sure he is deep down inside. They don't deserve to have to defend him yet again from the truth everyone else in our family already knows all too well.

My mother takes my hand and tugs me off to the side as everyone moves on to something else to talk about, thankfully. "Honey, that girl needs stable people around her. You're the most stable person I know. Why do you think I asked you to let your brother stay with you? Yes, I wanted some time alone with your father, but I also hoped you might rub off on him."

"That's not how things work, Mom," I say quietly, hating how the hope never fades from her beautiful eyes. "Not with Wilder and not with this Mia girl. If they wanted to be like me, they would be already."

She doesn't say another word, but even as that hope remains, I see disappointment begin to cloud her expression. Whether it's for the client I turned down or my brother, I have no idea.

BY THE TIME I GET BACK TO MY PLACE A FEW HOURS later, the discussion of Mia and her crazy life is a distant memory after a day of good times with my family. Falling back onto my bed, I hear Wilder turn up the music out in the living room, a sure sign he's planning to continue the party here tonight.

My phone rings, and I see it's VIP Security. Maybe I was too hasty in thinking they'd never offer me another assignment again.

"Liam, it's Jonah Bradley. I can offer fifty percent more in pay and a bonus of ten grand to take the job."

"The Mia job? You still haven't found anyone to take that assignment?" I ask, stunned I can't stop this woman's name from invading my life once again.

"Yeah. Fifty percent more than your usual pay and a ten grand bonus the second you say yes. So will you do it?"

Instantly, the word no forms on my lips, but then all that stuff my mother said about Mia needing stable people around her comes back to me. Maybe I could help her.

"Fine. Fifty percent more and ten grand right now and I'll do it. But you better warn them. I'm not taking this job to be just another clown in the Mia circus. I take my job seriously, so I expect them to understand I'm there to handle security like a professional."

"Great! I'll be sure to tell her mother that. She's her manager, so she's the one you'll be dealing with, for the most part. She returned back home two days ago, so you'll need to meet with them at her home tomorrow to get things going. I'll have my assistant send you the details. Make it late morning. She likes to sleep in."

"The mother or the superstar?" I ask, not trying to temper my snideness.

"Both. Good luck, and remember I have the utmost faith in you."

I toss my phone beside me onto the bed and let out a heavy sigh as Wilder's music fills the room around me. Christ, I hope I haven't made a mistake. The last thing I need in my life is a diva like Mia.

What are the chances she's going to like having a by the book security chief?

CHAPTER THREE

ia

MY HEAD SPINS AT HOW MANIPULATIVE MY MOTHER can be. Why I ever agreed to make her my manager is beyond me. Isn't there some law against sixteen year old girls signing legal contracts or something?

Four hours of fighting with her has left me drained and utterly unable to remember a single good moment in my life. The relaxing couple of days I stole feel like a distant memory, something I heard about once from someone but never actually experienced.

"I'm not going to explain myself, Mother. I needed time away. I'm done here," I say before turning on my heel and heading toward my room.

In my home. On my estate. Perhaps she needs to be reminded of that.

Behind me, my mother says in a low voice, "And

one more thing. Michael's been fired. I hired another chief of security, one who hopefully understands the basic tenets of his job and doesn't confuse himself with your BFF. He'll be here today."

Every inch of my body stills in complete shock. Michael fired? She wouldn't do that.

Slowly, I turn around to face her as everything in the living room fades away, leaving only the two of us standing in a sea of white rage that surrounds me. "Don't. He doesn't deserve to be fired, so whatever you did, undo it now, Mother, or I swear to God, you'll regret it."

My mother's usually placid expression, courtesy of Botox, twists into an angry scowl. "He's gone, Mia. You don't need more people around you giving into every silly whim you have. You need someone who's going to do his job. Period. If you want someone to be a friend, then find a friend, but Michael's gone."

My heart pounds like a jackhammer in my chest. My mother's done terrible things before, but never has she done anything like this. Firing Michael is something I can't forgive. She's gone too far this time.

"Rehire him, or I will never perform again," I say flatly, desperately trying to keep myself balanced as every emotion inside me threatens to explode all over her.

"No. It's done and that's that. The new man Jonah over at VIP recommended will be here in a few minutes, so make yourself presentable and try to remember that unlike you, the rest of the world is just trying to do their jobs."

That's it. I can't keep anything in check anymore, so I scream, "I will never perform another show if you don't bring him back!"

Casually, she shrugs and sits down to drink her morning energy shake. "You wouldn't do that. You love singing."

I march over to where she sits doling out her unjust punishments for people I care about and scream, "I used to love singing. Now I hate it!"

She opens her mouth to say something else that will set me off, but just then, I see my mother's assistant Candy walk in with a man who towers over her. He's got to be six and a half feet, and he's built like a brick wall. Worst of all, he doesn't smile or even look happy to be here.

This is my new chief of security? I don't fucking think so.

"Oh, no! You replaced Michael with him? Nope!"

My mother's expression turns to one of pure horror, likely because she thinks I offended some ridiculous code of conduct she believes everyone should follow. I'm not going to be polite if I don't agree with something, and I definitely don't agree with having that miserable giant guarding me.

Why doesn't anyone understand there has to be a relationship between two people who work together? Michael was someone who cared about me. This guy looks like the Marines just let him go because he crushed his entire platoon with his bare hands.

I storm out and head up to my bedroom where at least I can be left alone and think. There has to be some way to get Michael back and that guy the hell out of here. I'm the goddamn moneymaking machine here, not my mother. She can't do this. I'm not some underage little girl who needs her help anymore. I'm a grown adult who isn't taking this shit anymore from her or anyone else.

As I pace back and forth across my bedroom floor, I can't help but be curious about what she's saying down there. I open the door a crack and listen for her usual nonsense about how we run a professional company and all that garbage.

Nothing happens here without me. Why is it she's forgotten that?

I strain to hear her talking, but eventually a few words begin drifting up the stairs. "I'm sorry. She's not herself this morning. Mia really isn't like this. Really."

Then the gigantic guy speaks, and I can barely contain my rage.

"I'm sure. I'm Liam Jackson. Jonah Bradley convinced me that I'm the man for this job. To be honest, I'm not so sure."

What kind of attitude is that? Who hired this jackass?

But of course, my mother is more than happy to ease his worries. "Trust me, my daughter is a wonderful person. Honestly. Plus, if Jonah believes you're the right man for the job, then I believe it too, Liam. Would you like something to eat or maybe some juice?"

Now she's offering him breakfast? Oh, no. Not happening.

I march downstairs to find the two of them chatting like they're the best of friends. "Sorry to break up this little morning coffee klatsch thing you have going on, but if anyone is going to interview prospective employees, it's me."

Turning toward the oversized thing in front of me, I march right up to him and size him up, starting from his feet. He's taller than Michael, but that doesn't mean he's any good at his job. In fact, it might mean he's like a big, bumbling clown who can't move fast if danger approaches.

Still, I feel like it takes my eyes forever to travel up his long legs and those black dress pants. Nice chest in that mint green dress shirt, although that doesn't have to be a good thing. Clearly, this lug works out.

"What makes you qualified to protect the likes of someone at my level?" I ask.

As I wait for his answer, my gaze drifts over his arms and I can't help but wonder how big those biceps are. Does he live in the gym? That's not going to happen if he works for me. I'm not paying some guy to be a gym rat. Let him do that on his own time.

When I look up at his face, I see nothing but disgust in his expression, which pisses me off. This could be the best gig in the world for someone like him, and he looks like he wants to throw up.

Nice attitude there, bud.

But his eyes are the bluest shade of blue I've ever seen, and next to his dark brown, nearly black hair, they seem to sparkle. Nice. Then again, what the hell does it matter what a bodyguard's eyes look like? As long as they see anything that could hurt me, I don't care what color they are.

Even if they're literally the most gorgeous eyes I've ever seen.

I take one final glance at him in total, noticing he's got great shoulders, but I can't let myself get distracted by that. It's not hard to get shoulders like that. Michael had nice shoulders. Hell, I've seen hundreds of men who have shoulders that look like this guy's. It's nothing terribly special. Just comes from some working out. Nothing special about that.

He doesn't look like anyone who would listen to my music, which is a huge problem. Even worse, the way he stares down at me but says nothing to answer my very simple question irritates me. This guy wants to work for me but thinks he can look at me with disdain?

Oh, no, pal. No way.

"Mia, it's clear the man is qualified," my mother says as he and I continue our staring match.

I don't tear my gaze away as I hold up my hand to stop her. "No. I want him to tell me, not you. I'm the goddamned client here. I'm the one he'll be expected to protect, so I'm the one he needs to answer."

But still he says nothing.

Staring me down, he finally clears his throat after nearly a minute passes of us staring at one another and says in a deep voice, "I've worked for Senator Stanford, the head of Cititrust, and an actress you may know, Angela Manning."

Still refusing to break the stare, I say, "Not a single

one of those people are anywhere as big as me."

He shrugs, and for the first time, I see a hint of a smile that does nothing but infuriate me more. "Senator Stanford was a pretty beefy guy. Even bigger than you."

I step back from him and turn to glare at my mother. "A funny guy? Exactly the one thing in a man you know I hate."

"Then I guess it's a good thing I'm not here for that," he says smugly.

I snap my attention back to him to see him grinning. Who the hell does this guy think he is?

"Mia, he's exactly who we need," my mother says in her soft, social worker voice that never fails to enrage me. I hate when she attempts to handle me like this. "Give him a chance."

Now I swivel my head to look over at her and bark, "Who we need? Are you now famous and need a bodyguard? I'm struggling to think of a single manager anyone ever gave a damn about."

I'm not interested in hearing another word from either of these people, so I march back to my room and slam the door. I had a head of security I could trust. Michael cared about me. We were friends. We were more than friends. He wasn't only a bodyguard who was willing to go behind my mother's back and let me have the happiness I so desperately crave. He was someone who truly cared for me.

And now my mother has sent him away just like she sends everyone away.

I grab my phone off my dresser and call Michael.

He'll know what to do. He always does. He'll have a plan that will make this all better. Then my mother will see that I don't need Mr. Big and Rude downstairs. I just need the one person I can trust to protect me like he always has since I was sixteen.

My heart sinks as I hear his phone ring and ring and then my call goes to voicemail. I listen to his gentle voice tell me to leave a message, reveling in the sound of a familiar, friendly soul who cares about me.

With tears welling in my eyes, I say, "Michael, it's Mia. I know my mother fired you, but I can undo that. Call me so we can figure out what to do next. I miss you."

Falling back onto the bed, I hold my phone to my chest and wait for him to call back. He never makes me wait more than a minute or two. That's one of the things I love about him. He always shows that I'm his number one priority, unlike everyone else around me.

One minute turns to two and then turns to five. I lift my phone in front of me to see if it rang and I didn't hear it, but there are no missed calls. Maybe he's stuck in traffic. Or in a tunnel. Or somewhere there's shitty reception. That happens a lot.

I think back to that one time he and I had to go to one of those home stores to get him a new shower curtain. I'd never been in one of them before that day, and I was so thrilled to find out that a simple blond wig and sunglasses made it possible for me to walk around like any other person looking for tools or shower curtains. When I tried to call my mother, though, I couldn't get a call out, and Michael explained that the metal construction of the building made it hard to use cell phones there.

That's probably why he hasn't called back yet. He always knew the answer to why things happened like they did. That's what I need. Not some giant, angry guy who thinks this job is some kind of demotion for him. I need a friend like Michael who cared and answered my questions, no matter how stupid they were because I've experienced so little in life.

After ten minutes, I try to call him again, but this time it goes directly to voicemail. His phone never does that. Why would it go directly to voicemail?

Mine only does that if I turn it off or I decline a call. Did he deliberately not answer my call? He has to know it's me. My name comes up right in the middle of his screen with that picture of me he took that time on the ride back from a show in Oklahoma City.

Why would he not want to talk to me?

TEN MINUTES LATER, AFTER CHARMING THE GUY AT the front gate and the helpful assistance of an Uber driver, I stand outside of Michael's apartment feeling like I'm about to unravel. Michael has never not answered one of my calls. He knows how much I depend on him to keep me sane when my mother insists on constantly making my life a living hell.

So why didn't he answer?

A second after I knock, I hear noises inside his apartment. It sounds like there's more than one person in there. Maybe his sister came over to visit when she heard he got fired. After helping me, she's probably going to be pissed, but I'll tell her like I plan to tell Michael that I'm going to get him his job back. He doesn't have to worry about that. I won't let my mother get away with this latest stunt of hers.

The door opens, and finally, I see a friendly face. "Michael! Why didn't you answer my call? I tried like half a dozen times."

He leans against the doorframe and quickly buttons his jeans, like I caught him right after getting out of the shower. Except he doesn't look like he's clean at all. If anything, he looks pretty nasty right now, as if he's been drinking ever since he found out what my mother did.

"My phone's been on the fritz. You know how it is. I should have gotten a new one a while ago."

I push past him to walk into his place, wrinkling my nose at the stench that hits me not two steps in. "I needed to come over and tell you I won't let my mother get away with firing you. She had no right, and I told her that. So, you don't have to worry. You'll have your job back today. I promise."

"Mia…"

With a shake of my head, I stop him. He doesn't have to say a word. None of this is his fault. I was the one who asked him to get me that hotel room, and I was the one who asked him to help me sneak away. He doesn't deserve to pay for merely doing as I wanted.

"It's okay, Michael. I won't let her do it. She brought some big guy in to replace you this morning, but I've already put my foot down and told her no way am I letting that happen. Just give me a few hours and you'll be back at the house where you belong."

A noise that sounds like someone snickering comes from the bathroom, and Michael nervously glances in that direction as I try to understand the vibe I'm getting from this place. He hasn't been drinking away his sadness at losing his job. There are no empty beer bottles, and that's all Michael drinks.

And that smell isn't stale alcohol. It's weed and something else, but I can't seem to place it.

"Mia, you should go. I'm sure everyone's looking for you by now, so you should go," he says as he begins to guide me toward the front door.

Why is he giving me the bum's rush like this? We're friends. We sit together every night and talk about everything. Why does he want me to go so soon?

"I don't want to go yet. I miss you, Michael. I want you back as my security guy. I feel safe with you."

Again, a sound like someone's in the bathroom laughing hits my ears, and I see Michael's eyes get wide. He heard it too.

"What's going on here?" I ask as I look around at the mess of his apartment. "Why does it feel like you haven't been sitting here all sad about losing your job protecting me?"

Then I smell that scent I couldn't place a minute ago and finally know what it is. Sex.

"Mia, just go and whatever happens, it's okay," Michael says sheepishly.

My emotions begin to unravel inside me. I thought

he cared about me. I thought we were friends. God, I thought we were more than friends.

I thought Michael and I were soulmates.

But one day after my mother fired him, he's here getting high and sleeping with someone? Even worse, he doesn't want to admit it and simply wants me to leave, to get out of his hair so he can go back to banging this woman?

"It's not okay!" I say, my voice breaking out into a sob as I storm over to the bathroom door to fling it open.

A blonde with ratty hair in a pink tank top and a baby puke green thong looks at me like I'm the skank and giggles again. "Who the fuck is she?"

Almost as if he's irritated he has to introduce us, Michael grumbles, "Mia, this is Tracey. Tracey, Mia."

The skeevy girl tilts her head to the side and gives me a crooked smile. "Hey."

I feel the tears begin to burn the backs of my eyes and hate that this is how my body chooses to react to the news that the one person I thought truly cared for me doesn't give a damn about losing his job or being removed from my life. Michael wasn't my soulmate. He wasn't even someone who missed me enough not to hook up with this nasty girl with bad taste in clothes.

"Mia, it's not like we were…"

His sentence trails off as I march past him toward the front door. I know what he doesn't have the balls to say to my face. It's not like we were together.

He's right. We weren't. I never slept with him

because after the mess of my life for the past year, I wanted to be sure someone cared for me before I took that step again. After Jonny, I thought I needed that, and I thought Michael understood.

I thought a lot of things that obviously weren't true.

God, I'm such a fool!

"Goodbye, Michael. Enjoy your life here with her," I say, choking back the tears.

So much for him being my soulmate. All those nights we spent talking meant nothing to him. All the things I shared with him were simply part of his job, obviously.

With one last look back at Michael, I see Tracey walk up behind him and wrap her arms around his waist like she wants to show me he's hers. She doesn't have to worry. I'm a fool, but I'm not stupid. She can have him.

He was never anything to me anyway. At least, he never thought he was. The problem is I did think he was someone special.

My tears make running down the steps away from his apartment next to impossible, and I stumble as I hurry toward the bottom floor of the building. Crashing into the wall next to the stairs, I steady myself and wipe my eyes.

God, I was so stupid! Jonny told me when we broke up that no one was ever going to love me. That I wasn't enough for anyone to deal with all the bullshit that comes with me.

Now I know he was right.

CHAPTER FOUR

iam

ANDREA SETS A MUG OF COFFEE DOWN ON THE table in front of me as I sit back on the sofa, already regretting my choice to take this assignment after that little outburst of Mia's. Her mother, along with her assistant, wear uncomfortable expressions and talk in hushed tones over near the doorway before Andrea returns alone to sit across from me in what looks like a chair that should be in a museum instead of a living room.

She eases down onto the blood red upholstered seat and instantly appears even more uncomfortable than just a few moments ago. Not surprising, I guess, considering it looks to be some antique from hundreds of years ago. The dark wood ornate legs and arms remind me of something Santa Claus used to sit in at the mall when I'd go see him as a little boy.

Cradling a mug of coffee in her hands, she says, "You know, this life can be very hard, especially for someone like Mia. She's had a lot to adjust to. The stardom and fame. That kind of thing. She's actually a wonderful person. I just want you to know that so you don't think she's always like she was before. Things have just been difficult recently."

I have no idea what to say to that since I doubt this woman wants my true opinion of her daughter, so I force a smile and nod. "I'm sure."

That's all it takes to get her talking, and I let her tell me how Mia wanted to sing since she was a little girl and how they did the pageant circuit and she was crowned Little Miss Tampa. Andrea practically beams pride as she talks, and I want to believe the person I met a short time ago isn't the petty tyrant she appears to be.

But it's going to take more than a stroll down memory lane to convince me of that.

"Everyone who saw her perform as a little girl in those pageants told me she had something rare. I knew it, but hearing them say it made me think we should try to see how far it could go. So she started entering talent contests. You know the local ones you see advertised online and on posters at the mall? They weren't anything big at first, but then when she was fourteen, she won a contest and the prize was studio time. It was like a dream come true for her...for all of us, and from there, she took off like a comet. By the time she was fifteen, she had a number one hit. But it's a hard thing to get used to being famous, and she's so young, so that makes it doubly hard."

I get the sense that she's going to continue singing her daughter's praises, and I'm not in the mood to listen to any more of that. After taking a sip of the weakest coffee I've ever tasted in my life, I lean forward to set the mug back down on the table and level my gaze on her.

"I'm sorry if this is out of line, but no one, no matter how big, has a right to speak to people like that."

Andrea doesn't miss a beat and immediately defends her daughter once more. Drawing her eyebrows in, she looks truly pained when she says, "She's my only child. Her father and I couldn't have any more. When she said she wanted to be a singer, I devoted everything in my power to make that happen. Her father couldn't handle that, so he walked away five years ago. It's only been Mia and me ever since."

As much as I want to sympathize with her, that isn't my job. I need her to understand that the reason Jonah Bradley thought I was the right man for this position is because I'm not someone who falls apart at a sob story.

Changing the subject, I say, "About her last security chief. She obviously had a relationship with him above and beyond what it was supposed to be."

I'm surprised when she shakes her head and waves that little bit of truth away. "Oh, that was nothing. She's had to spend a lot of time on the road in the past couple years. It gets lonely. Michael fell for her like everyone does. I don't blame him. Mia's a flirt, like most young girls, so people can't help but fall in love with her."

A flirt? I haven't seen that part of her yet, obviously. She talks like her daughter is Venus or some mythical creature with the power to enchant all who come into her presence. I can't imagine how anyone could stand being in the same room with her for more than a few minutes, much less sleep with her. Sure, she's beautiful, possibly more beautiful than any woman I've ever met before, but she's awful and thoughtless to the people who care the most about her.

And that's downright ugly.

"I think I better go see how Mia's doing. I'll be right back. Please, make yourself at home. When I get back, we'll get everything straightened out about where you'll sleep and all of that."

She walks out of the room, leaving me to wonder if I want to stay here long enough to have to sleep. Right now, I feel like calling Jonah and telling him there's no amount of money he can pay me and no bonus big enough to make me want to stick around and deal with Mia's bullshit.

While I try to think of any reason why I should live up to my word, Andrea runs back into the room frantically waving her arms. "She's not in her room. She's gone again! My car is here, so I don't know where she could be."

Without thinking, I shift into work mode. I stand up and gently take her by the shoulders to calm her down. "Where would she go? Think of where you see her running to."

Andrea shakes her head and begins to cry. "I don't know. God, I should have never let her storm out of here like that. I should have followed her immediately."

"Listen to me. She doesn't have that much of a lead on us, so think about where she would go to. There has to be a place she'd want to be. A favorite spot somewhere? She can't be that far."

That calms her down and she begins to nod like she understands we have to use common sense to get through this. "Michael's. She'd go find him. He has an apartment in Tampa."

"Okay. Let's go there."

SHE PULLS UP TO AN APARTMENT COMPLEX AT THE address she has for Mia's former head of security and one glance at the place horrifies her. "Why would he live in a place like this? He made good money working for my daughter. This place looks like somewhere drug addicts hang out when they can't find their usual terrible spot."

I look out the window at the rundown tan buildings in front of me and wonder something similar myself. Nobody who has any decent income would live in a place with junk cars strewn about, broken glass in windows, and screen doors hanging off their frames.

As much as I'd like to imagine what this Michael's

deal is, we don't have time to solve that mystery. "What's the apartment number?"

"Two seventy-three."

I open the car door and start to move. "Then let's go visit apartment two seventy-three and see what Michael has to say."

By the time we reach the door to the apartment, I'm sure I've seen half a dozen health code violations, and that's not counting the empty syringes tossed along the dead flower beds that line the sidewalks. This place isn't the Ritz, for sure.

"God, I hope she's not in there," Andrea whispers as I rap my knuckles off the wood door.

The number three comes loose from the door and drops down so it looks like we're standing in front of apartment two seven E. Andrea and I glance over at one another, and I can't help but think that's an ominous sign.

Christ, I hope I don't have to rush the client to the hospital on my first day at this job. I was hoping to ease into the madness, not jump in head first.

The door opens to reveal a shirtless man in a pair of faded ripped jeans he didn't bother to zip up all the way. His dark hair is sticking up like someone's been running their hands through it, and by the odor of funk coming off him, he and whoever he's spending his time with in there have been smoking some stink weed and getting busy.

Trying not to breathe in, I ask, "Where's Mia?"

Beside me, Andrea says in a voice full of fear,

"Michael, did she come here? Is she in there with you?"

A half-naked blond woman wearing only a too-small pink tank top and a green thong inches up behind Michael. Sliding her hands around his waist, she strokes up and down his body, her chipped red fingernails getting lost in his chest hair, and asks in a sleepy voice, "Who is it now, baby?"

He turns to look at her and then back at me. With a shrug, he answers, "She left. When she saw Tracey, she ran out."

I look away in disgust and start pushing Andrea down the hallway. "Let's go. We need to move fast."

"Where could she be?" she asks as I guide her toward the stairs.

"I don't know, but we'll be faster in a car than she is on foot, assuming she didn't get into a cab or an Uber."

By the time we reach the car, Andrea's winded, so I jump in behind the wheel. "Is there anywhere she likes to go when she's upset?" I ask as I pull away from the curb.

As she tries to catch her breath, she shakes her head. "I don't know. I swear to God this child is going to kill me. I don't think I've ever run that fast in my life."

I take the turn out of Michael's apartment complex sharp, sending Andrea sliding across her seat and nearly crashing into me. "Think. Anywhere she'd feel better."

Pushing herself upright, she says, "When she was a

little girl, whenever she got sad, she'd go outside and sit under a tree we had in the backyard. But that was years ago."

"Where's the house?" I ask as I take another hard turn, this time to the right.

"St. Augustine."

Not helpful. I doubt she's making her way back across the state to sit under some damn tree in someone else's yard. Maybe her comment isn't entirely useless, though.

"I'm going to look for a park. I'm thinking maybe Mia has a thing for nature when she gets unhappy."

"That might be a good idea!"

Five minutes later, I pull up to a park and scan the area. No sign of her.

As I jump out of the car, I order Andrea to take the right side of the grass. "We'll cover more ground if we split up. You go over there and check out that side of the park. I'll take this side over here."

She hurries away while I take off running in the opposite direction, my eyes scanning every inch of the grass and trees in front of me. Thankfully, even though it's a beautiful day out, very few people have chosen to come to this park today.

I consider yelling Mia's name, but that would likely make her bolt in the opposite direction. She and I didn't get off on the best foot this morning, so I doubt she's going to be thrilled to see me.

Tree after tree passes in front of my eyes, but no Mia. After ten minutes, I'm about to give up and see if Andrea had any more success than I did when I spy a figure beneath a tree at the back of the park near a fence. The young woman's dark brown hair hangs over her face, but I recognize the black and pink yoga pants Mia was wearing back at the house. She's huddled with her arms around her knees and looks nothing like the person who chewed off my head and her mother's not an hour ago.

I stop a few feet in front of her and quietly say her name so as not to frighten her. "Mia."

She doesn't look up, but when she speaks, the pain in her voice comes through loud and clear. "I thought he cared. He's gone for one day and it's like we were never anything but strangers."

"We should go. Someone's going to recognize you here if we don't."

That makes her lift her head, and I can't help but be struck at how genuinely sad she looks now. And how fragile compared to just a short while ago.

"I know what you're probably thinking. That it was just sex. Well, it wasn't. We never even slept together. It was deeper than that. Michael listened to me. He understood me. Or at least I thought he did."

Tears well in her eyes, but I don't stop myself from giving her my honest opinion of her friend. "Your buddy doesn't strike me as an understanding kind of guy."

She shoots me a nasty look. "Go away."

Taking a step closer to her, I try to imagine how it feels to be let down by that dirtbag when I'm one of the biggest stars in the world. But I can't do it. I don't know what she saw in that guy, but whatever it was, it didn't actually exist.

"Mia, I'm hired to protect you. You're not safe here."

Confusion fills her expression, and she shakes her head. "What do you care?"

Scanning the area for any potential danger, I force a smile. "I care because it's my job. Now let's go."

I'm not sure which part of that convinces her it's time to leave her spot under the tree, but she reluctantly stands up and I quickly step closer to her to shield her from anything that might be lurking nearby. She tilts her head back and glares up at me like she did back at the house.

"You're going to want to work on that caring you supposedly do. This feels more like you're a cop and I'm your prisoner."

As I look down into her dark eyes full of fury for me, I think to myself that I should have listened to my gut and walked away from this job last night. This is what I get for listening to my mother and her wishful thinking.

CHAPTER FIVE

ia

For a week, I've had to get used to this new security guy. Liam. He's pleasant enough, I guess, if you have a thing for authoritarian rulers and the straight and narrow. Like don't step a toe out of line or you're in big trouble kind of straight and narrow. If that gets a girl going, then I imagine he's nothing short of a god to that type of person.

For me, he's just standoffish enough to make me miss Michael every so often, and then I remember what he looked like the last time I saw him standing in his apartment with that floozy hanging off him like some sloppy, hand-me-down, ugly coat. No smile or attempt to stop me so I might think he cared. No hug like he used to give me whenever he came back from a day away.

Nothing but what looked like irritation that I showed up to interrupt his fucking with little miss skank.

As I lay on my bed and stare up at the ceiling, I remember why I love being out on the road so much. Everything is new, every city is different, and you never have to focus on what happened before because something interesting is right around the corner. Here it's the same thing every day.

Deal with my mother.

Be practically ignored by the bodyguard I pay to protect me.

Hide out in my room and pretend like any of this is normal.

If only I hadn't told the crew to take a few days off. At least if they were here, I'd have someone to talk to.

I'm sure my mother has instructed the new guy to stay away from me. God forbid a man pay any attention to me. Unless, of course, he's in the audience far enough away to never touch me and has bought a ticket for the pleasure of getting a look at me.

Nothing like feeling as if you're only one step up from being in the tent on the edge of the circus where they keep the bearded lady and other freaks.

God, I'm so restless. At least when Michael was around, I had someone to laugh with and watch old TV shows with. Now, I'm alone until my entourage returns from their vacation.

That leaves me with my mother, her idiot assistant,

and Liam to entertain me. Things don't look good for the immediate future, sadly.

I get up off the bed and wander over to the window to look out at the grounds. I could go swimming. No. There's nothing sadder than one person swimming, unless they're exercising, and I'm officially not doing that until my trainer forces me back into the gym.

Maybe a walk around the property. God, no. As if I haven't seen every square inch of this estate. Little of it is what I want it to look like anyway. My mother and the gardener make all those decisions. I merely get to pose in front of the meticulously trimmed topiaries or whatever beautiful flowers they choose this season whenever some media outlet wants an in-depth look into the private life of Mia.

It's all a façade, but whatever sells, I guess.

Wanderlust courses through my veins, but after bolting from under my mother's watchful eye twice in the past week, I doubt I'd have any success trying to sneak out again. Maybe if Michael was still around, but with General Liam on duty, forget it.

As my gaze roams over the colorful flower gardens and the perfectly manicured green grass, I wonder if it's possible to tunnel out. Those prisoners did it from Alcatraz, right? If they could dig through rock, I certainly could dig through some sandy Florida land that sits beneath the sod.

Except by the time I actually got anywhere good, it would be time to head out onto the road again, so all of my work would be for nothing. Kudos to you, Mia, for thinking outside the box, though. Just for that, you get to spend another boring day all alone.

Out of the corner of my eye, I see Liam walk out toward the gardens. From the back of the property, my head of security for the estate Javier walks toward him. I've always liked Javier. He's quiet but never fails to have a smile for me, unlike the new guy whose face looks like it might break if he tried to be nice and show me his pearly whites.

For a few seconds, I wonder what they're talking about, but something about the way Liam's dressed takes over my thoughts. His black T-shirt only serves to make his biceps look bigger than when I first met him wearing a dress shirt. I wonder if he's been spending all his off time in the gym. He must. Nobody looks that built naturally. Unlike that first day, now he's in jeans, and as much as I want to see him as merely an officious bastard of my mother's, I can't deny he's good-looking.

Then I zero in on something just peeking out from under his sleeve. Is that a tattoo? It's black, so maybe it's only his shirt. I can't tell, but it looks like a tattoo. I wonder what he's got a tattoo of. I didn't think he had that level of cool in him.

Go figure.

Tall, silent, possibly tattooed, and hot. Like some kind of disapproving statue of a modern Adonis that roams around my home saying as few words as possible to me.

Is he like Michael? Does he just say things because

that's what he's expected to do but doesn't care at all about my welfare? Because clearly that's what my former head of security truly felt about me.

My thoughts meander from Michael back to my new security chief, and I can't help but wonder about this guy. What's Liam's life like when he's not walking around looking disgruntled here?

I watch him stand perfectly straight as he and Javier talk, Liam towering over him by more than a few inches. How tall is the new guy? I guessed maybe six and a half feet tall that first day, but now I'm thinking he might be even taller than that.

Did he play basketball in high school? He seems like he'd be tall enough, and he is pretty built. It's not like he's one of those stick guys who are really tall but don't have an ounce of fat on them. I hate those guys. I've always imagined sleeping with one of them would be like having sex with a rake. Definitely not something I want to experience.

My mind drifts to a place where I wonder what sex with Liam would be like. Certainly not like banging a garden tool. There's a lot to hang on to with those muscular shoulders and arms. I stare out my window and try to make out what his abs look like under that black T-shirt. I bet he's got washboard abs. Michael had a nice body, but he didn't have great abs. I used to tease him about being flabby in the middle all the time. I don't imagine I'd ever get to say that to Liam.

Suddenly, I realize what I'm doing. Why the hell am I imagining the new guy's body under his clothes?

I don't even like him. He's sullen and bossy, and to be honest, I'm not even sure he has the ability to smile. Maybe those are the muscles he should work out more often.

Mumbling to myself, I stare at him and say, "Yeah, maybe try a few lifts of the corners of your mouth, miserable bastard. You might not look so disgusted all the time."

I know why he looks that way. It's me. He doesn't approve of me or how I act or what I say. Well, fuck him. I don't need his approval. I get that from millions of people around the world. Who the hell cares what some bodyguard on loan from my mother's favorite place to get them thinks of me?

Javier laughs, and my attention is drawn to Liam's reaction to another person being happy. For the first time, I see him smile—a genuine smile with teeth that makes him look really sweet, not the forced kind he gives me whenever I walk into a room, like he knows he has to tolerate me and he's been told that includes being nice, but he never really gets his mouth turned up enough to look anything but irritated.

So Liam can smile and be happy. Just not around me.

Does he have a wife? Girlfriend? Maybe that's why he's been so cool to me. He has someone back home waiting for him.

Where is home? I thought I heard my mother say to her assistant that he's from the Tampa area. He probably lives in a nice little house with a pretty blond woman who has long legs and doesn't have to crane her neck to look up at him. They have a three-bedroom home with one bath and a half bath the previous owner put in, but they like the place and figure it will work until kids come.

Or does he have kids already?

I shake my head and push that thought away. No man with a beautiful wife and little kids would leave that behind to come work for me. The one day a week he has off when I'm not on the road wouldn't be enough to sustain a relationship, and the weeks and months away from those he loves, even for the amount he's getting paid, wouldn't be worth it.

I mean, for God's sake, it's not the fucking Depression. A guy like him could find work anywhere.

So no kids, but I bet he has a girlfriend or wife. No guy with a body like that and good looks stays single for long. My gaze travels up and down those faded jeans as he and Javier walk around the grounds.

Maybe he's a player. A different woman every night of the week.

That thought makes me chuckle. No way this guy is sleeping with a different woman every night. No way, no how. He's too much a follow the rules type. Those guys are never manwhores. Men like Liam are the steady kind of guys. They don't sleep around on someone if they care about them.

The way he is may sound boring to a lot of woman, but I can see how it would be really great to have a man like that. I've had the other kind, and that made me feel like shit, so maybe it could be nice to have a stable, steady man.

His girlfriend probably knows that, though. She likes how reliable he is and how secure he makes her feel. She's smart in that way. She likely is intelligent. Beautiful with a good head on her shoulders. I can see him going for someone like that. Not flashy. Just classically beautiful and sweet.

I look over toward the mirror on the far wall and see the last remnants of the purple dye job from a couple months ago peeking out from underneath the disheveled dark brown mess on top of my head that's the result of not bothering to do anything with my hair this morning. Definitely not classically beautiful. More like startlingly appealing to some men who like their women to look like a cross between Medusa and Lady Gaga.

Liam's girlfriend definitely looks forward to seeing him when he walks through the door. Why wouldn't she? I mean, he's got a great body, and I imagine if he actually likes a person, he could be quite pleasant to be around.

I watch him and Javier stop near that ridiculous plant my mother insisted we have in the garden last year. Big and flashy with bright pink floppy petals that remind me of elephant ears, it looks like a flower that requires constant attention or it will wither away and die. No wonder my mother loved it when the landscaper suggested it.

What does it feel like to have someone to look forward to seeing? I've never had that in my life. No one I've ever been with made me look forward to seeing them. They were simply always around, and then one day, they weren't.

Clearly, I've never loved anyone, and I doubt anyone's ever loved me because I don't think any of the guys I've been with could honestly say they looked forward to seeing me. Anticipation isn't really a thing when you're going full tilt, twenty-four seven in a relationship.

But that's lust. That's not love. I might not have much experience with love, well none actually, but I know what it's supposed to feel like. I sing about it in practically every song I perform.

Love is supposed to thrill you but comfort you. It's supposed to make you think the world doesn't suck, even while it still does way too damn often, because at the end of the day after all is said and done, you have someone who truly cares about your happiness to come home to.

That's what love is. Not hearts and flowers but the knowledge deep inside that whatever the world throws at you, no matter how bad it gets, you have someone covering your back and worrying if you're okay or not.

I bet that's what Liam's girlfriend feels all the time. It's the reason she fell in love with him. It certainly couldn't be because he's a scintillating conversationalist or someone who makes her laugh all the time. No, it's because whenever life gets her down, she only has to look behind her to see him watching and making sure no one ever hurts her.

He's good at that kind of thing. That's probably

why he works as a bodyguard. He said he cares because it's his job, but I think he protects people because that's who he is. His girlfriend loves that about him. Everyone loves that about him. A big guy choosing not to be some jackass bully and pushing everyone around but protecting people instead, even when he can crush them like a bug? People love that.

I can see why, though. I mean, the world has way too many oversized asshole guys, so when you come upon someone like Liam, why wouldn't someone think he's pretty great?

Assuming they don't have to deal with his utter disdain every time he's in front of them.

Lost in my thoughts about his perfect life with the woman he loves, I don't see him looking up at me until he waves his hand. I focus on him and see no smile. Just a mixture of curiosity and disgust coming off him.

As always.

Sneering, I turn away, partly embarrassed that he caught me staring at him and partly annoyed at this perfect life he gets to return to when he doesn't have to be here barely tolerating me. His girlfriend probably greets him at the door like some submissive fifties housewife wearing pearls and a dress with her hair perfect.

Whatever. Not everyone can have that life. Some of us got stuck with something very different and don't get that lovey-dovey welcome every time we come through the door.

Not even from people who are supposed to be happy to see us.

Fuck, I need to get out of this house. I think I'm starting to go stir crazy.

Desperate to find anything to take my mind off my new bodyguard's perfect life, I head down to the kitchen to find something cool to drink. I might even go lay out near the pool. Doing that alone isn't pathetic like swimming all by yourself.

Thankfully, my mother and her assistant are nowhere to be found, so I can enjoy a glass of iced tea in peace and quiet. I take a big gulp and let it slide down my throat, loving how it cools everything on its way down. I swear if my mother comes storming in and launches into a lecture about how caffeine can be damaging to the vocal chords, I'm going to douse this entire room in my favorite drink and laugh as she stands there dripping from head to toe in the stuff.

After my second refreshing gulp, I hear voices and know my precious peace and quiet is soon ending. Unfortunately, I don't sneak away back up to my room fast enough to avoid hearing my mother and Liam having some discussion about security at the house here, and it doesn't take more than a few words to make me see red.

"I think the changes I've started to make to the security here at the estate will be a big improvement," he says with so much confidence that I want to charge out into the living room and ask the obvious question.

Why the hell do we have to change anything? What was wrong with the security the way it's always been here?

My mother, of course, loves the idea of changing

the security. She probably has him devising plans to see if a large wall around the property or a moat would be a good idea. Anything to keep me in where she can have her always-watchful eye on me.

"I appreciate you taking the time to assess the situation and make improvements, Liam. I knew Jonah made a good choice the first time I saw you," she gushes.

Cool your jets, Mom. He's half your age and has a perfect life to go home to, unlike the nightmare we have here.

Her fawning all over him sets my teeth on edge, and it's not long before I march out to confront both of them. I find my mother reclining on the white tuxedo sofa like some woman in a painting waiting for someone to come by with a large palm and start fanning her. Liam's standing a few feet away smiling at her like anything happening right now could be considered amusing.

How nice that both Javier and my mother have been on the receiving end of his happy smiles today.

When the two of them see me, all smiles disappear. Nice.

"You know, those people are professionals," I say to him, not bothering to discuss this with my mother. It isn't her money who pays everyone here.

"What makes you think you should be telling them how to do their jobs? Will you be instructing me on how to sing next?" I snap.

Liam looks dumbfounded for a few seconds. When

he finally speaks, I get the sense that he's not talking to me but to the room in general.

"Because we're all working toward the same goal," he says calmly, but that casual tone is forced. He likely wants to bark his opinion at me.

"Whatever I can do to help them I will, and they need to do whatever they can do to help me," he continues explaining.

It all sounds very logical, but I hate it.

"What was wrong with what they were doing before?" I ask, silently adding to myself that Michael had no issues with anything the people here did when he was my chief of security.

Of course, my mother has to jump in and try to help Liam, her new favorite person around here. "Mia, he's only trying to make sure you're the safest you can be. That's what we all want."

By the time she gets to her second comment, I know it's not only to help him. She's trying to handle me. God, I hate being handled.

I throw her a look that tells her I'm not in the mood for what she's trying to do, but Liam answers my question. "Nothing a little tightening can't fix. There's nothing wrong with making good even better."

Now he's trying to handle me too. I have to give him credit. He's a quick learner. It only took him just over a week to figure out how to do that.

Except I'm not playing that game today.

I take a few steps closer to him and stop dead when he glares down at me. Flustered, I snap, "You're trying to make my home a fortress to keep me trapped. I won't let you do that."

Once again, my mother tries to soothe my ruffled feathers, but I'm done playing nice with her today too. Spinning around to face her, I yell, "I ran away because I felt trapped. Why can't you understand that? I'm like a prisoner in my own home, and now you think more security is a good idea? Did anyone ever think to ask me how I feel about that? About anything?"

My outburst shocks my mother into silence, but not Liam. Behind me, he says, "Regardless of why you did it, running away put you in danger. It's my job to protect you, so there will be no more running. If you want to go somewhere, I'll be with you from now on."

Every word out of his mouth sounds more and more oppressive, so by the time I spin back around to face him, I don't even try to stop myself from getting in his face. I'm a foot shorter than he is, so it's not exactly like I'm in his face, but the intention is the same and he understands immediately, if the surprised look in his eyes is any indication.

Pointing my finger up at him, I square my shoulders and say, "I am not a child. I do not need you with me whenever I want to go anywhere. I am not the President's daughter, and you are not my Secret Service detail. If I want to go somewhere and I don't want you hanging on me, I'll decide what's going to happen, not you. You can follow behind where no one can see you so I can live my life as I please. That's how it will be from now on, Liam. If you don't like that, then don't let the door hit you on your way out."

I don't know why, but once I finish laying down the law for him, I don't storm out like I should since I can feel the tears welling up inside me, threatening to spill out all over the place and make me look like some overwrought teenage girl. Instead, I stand there staring up at him, unable to move.

For his part, he doesn't flinch either. We're like two enemy soldiers on the field of battle, neither of us willing to back down. Of course, the field of battle is my living room in my house and on my estate, so if I wanted to, I could simply have him removed from the premises.

Why I don't do that is something I truly don't understand. Let him go back to his perfect life with his perfect girlfriend who loves him because he's big, strong, and protective. I should just send him packing.

But I don't.

Or more correctly, I can't. Actually, it's I won't because I don't want to. I have no valid reason for wanting him to stay, but as I stand here staring up at him and he stares down at me, I think I'd miss having him around. It makes no sense. He's only been here for a little over a week, and he hasn't been nice to me a day of the time he's spent in my house.

Still, he's the only person in my world who refuses to back down. That intrigues me. I might be a masochist, but I like this standoff thing we're doing. It makes me feel more alive than I've felt since I stopped touring six months ago. Nothing has ever felt as invigorating as performing in front of a crowd.

Nothing until this thing with him.

When he sighs and looks away, a sense of victory washes over me. That round went to me. But I hope Liam doesn't give in that easily from now on.

Keep challenging me, Mr. Big and Serious. I don't know why, but I like it.

Next time, maybe I'll be the one to give in first. Wouldn't that be a change?

CHAPTER SIX

iam

ALONE IN MY ROOM ON THE OPPOSITE SIDE OF THE house away from my client, I hear a noise that sounds like people laughing. Since no one seems to do much of that in this place, I dismiss it, sure it's the sound from someone's TV.

When the laughter gets louder and then the sounds of what I think might be people dropping heavy things on the floor drowns out the fun, I head to the hallway to check on what's happening without putting on more clothes than the black basketball shorts and old T-shirt I'm wearing. If someone's breaking into the house, there isn't time for pants and shoes.

I barely make it out of my room before I see a hoard of people coming toward me. Five women and a man all around my age come strolling down the hallway with enough bags and luggage like they plan to stay for the rest of their lives. That explains the sounds I heard.

"Hey, who's the new guy?" a tall blond with legs that look to be almost as long as mine asks.

The six of them stop and stare at me while I wonder if I've been dropped into some way off Broadway production of a bad play Mia's decided to put on at the house here. When I don't answer after a few seconds, they appear to lose interest in who I am and keep walking down the hallway with what looks to be everything they own.

I watch as each of them walks into a room, except for two women who may be sisters or may just look very similar because of their short black hair and bright red lipstick. None of them close their doors, and for the next few minutes as I look on in shock, they float in and out of the rooms, laughing and singing, with the one who asked about me doing some kind of dance as she moves from one doorway to the next.

Since I'm sure I'm awake and not having some terrible nightmare, I decide to leave the cast of whatever shitty production this is and take a walk outside. It would have been nice if Andrea had told me to expect a cavalcade of boisterous people tonight.

As the minutes go by, they get louder and louder until I can't hear myself think. Who the hell are these people? I know they're with Mia, but are they friends or people who work for her? I had assumed there would be a bigger staff to handle all her needs, but since they never appeared over the past couple weeks, I guess I just forgot about them.

Now I don't think I'll ever be able to forget or even ignore them since they all seem to live at a decibel level akin to the sound of a jet taking off.

I stop at the pool and suddenly realize I can't hear them as much from here. Or maybe they've all been muzzled by security. That would be nice. Hell, that would be more than nice. It would be heavenly. I'd buy Javier and his guys a round of drinks for that.

But it only lasts for a few precious seconds before they start up again and sound like a pack of wild animals up there. Christ, how am I supposed to sleep with that racket right down the hall from me every night?

Taking a seat on the pool deck, I dangle my feet in the water and close my eyes as I cover my ears, desperate for a moment's peace. Now on top of a client who's two steps away from driving me nuts and her mother who's just a step behind her, there's this troupe of nonsense.

Unable to focus on anything, I hang my head and wish I could remember how much extra money I'm being paid for this assignment. The fact that I have to focus on that instead of the job is a clear indication this is not where I should be. I don't even need the goddamned money.

Why didn't I tell Jonah Bradley no instead of caving in after listening to my mother and her Pollyanna talk? I love the woman, but I swear to God in her world there are unicorns jumping over rainbows every day.

While I question nearly everything I've done since I said yes to this nightmare job, I hear someone say my name. Looking up, I see Mia standing next to me in jean shorts and a pink T-shirt. She says something, but between the noise and my hands over my ears, I can't hear her.

"Sorry, the circus came to town and set up shop in my hallway. Any chance you can get that to stop for the night and every night after that?" I yell up to her.

She doesn't answer but gives me a smile that tells me she thinks I'm making a big deal out of nothing. When she turns around and walks away, I figure I'm going to be stuck with this madness for the rest of my time here, which may not be long since a security chief who hasn't gotten any sleep night after night isn't much use to anyone. A minute later, though, everything falls silent.

Mia returns shortly after and sits down next to me on the pool deck, dangling her feet in the water like I do. Smiling again, she says, "I figured you for someone who insists on being asleep by ten. Sorry the crew woke you up."

"Yeah," I say, leaning back on my palms as the landscaping lights nearby throw shadows across the water in front of me.

"Is that yeah you prefer to go to sleep early or yeah for something else?" she asks with a chuckle.

When I don't answer since I'm not really in the mood for talking after dealing with her crew, she quietly says, "You don't think much of my lifestyle, do you?"

Tired of holding my tongue at this house, I turn to look at her and shake my head. "To be honest, no. Who are all those people and why do they act like that when they come to someone's home?"

"Well, Chloe and Ivy, the two women who look alike, they're my makeup artists. Crystal is my hair stylist. She's the one with the look that could turn a man to stone. I'm guessing you've seen that look already, though."

I try to remember if any of the women stared me down like she wanted to turn me to stone, but I can't recall that. Maybe I was too busy being in shock that they all thought they should traipse down the hallway in the middle of the night like they're at Mardi Gras.

Mia continues, "Mitchell is my personal trainer. I guess he's easy to figure out since he's the only man. Fair warning, he's got a thing for guys with great bodies, so don't be surprised if he hits on you."

"Sorry to disappoint Mitchell, but I'm straight."

She shrugs like my announcement means nothing. "He won't care. He has a type, and as far as I can tell, you're it. To be honest, he must be distracted tonight because if he was paying attention and saw you standing up there in those shorts, I know he would have made a move on you."

Fucking terrific. Yet another infuriating distraction in this house of madness.

"Tiffany is my choreographer, and Ainsley is my

life coach. Oh, and Ginger comes whenever I need new clothes. She's my personal shopper."

"I assume I've met Tiffany since there was at least one of the women dancing all the way down the hall," I say and then realize she just said one of those people was her life coach.

"What the hell is a life coach?" I ask, curious to know since I've heard people claim to need one more than a few times in the past.

"Ainsley helps me out with focusing on the positive."

I don't even try to hide how stupid I think that is. "Ainsley, the life coach who needs someone to clue her in that she should have manners enough to keep her voice down after midnight. Is she the one who sounds like she's birthing goats in her room right now? Because whatever that is, it's obnoxious. And why do you need hair and makeup people?"

My frustration seems to amuse Mia, and she smiles and shakes her head. "Men. They never understand the importance of hair and makeup. I need them so I don't look like some washed out hag on stage."

"Somehow I doubt you could ever look like a hag, but fair enough. Why do they live here, though? You've looked fine without them for weeks. On the road, I understand. Here? I don't get it."

"I'm surprised you have a problem with the Three Musketeers. I would have thought you'd look down your nose at Ainsley out of all of them."

Laughing at how easily she read me about that, I look up to see her life coach waving some item of clothing out her window. "I think she's trying some new moves your choreographer taught her. Either that or she thinks that's the way to get your attention. Whatever it is, I'm not seeing the use of a life coach."

Mia's expression turns serious, and she looks down at her feet in the water. "She's all that stood between me and losing it a while back. She makes me see my life has a lot of positive in it when I have a hard time finding it."

"You're a gorgeous woman with incredible talent and a voice millions of fans around the globe love, and you live on an estate that ninety percent of the people in this world can only dream of seeing, forget about owning. There. Now you can tell goat girl to go away and maybe I can get some sleep."

She turns to look at me with shock written all over her face for a long moment. I can't imagine why, although I doubt she's used to people talking to her like that. But it's not like anything I said wasn't true. She's all that and more. Why she needs some flaky woman to help her focus on the positive is beyond me.

"You…you can take one of the rooms in the east wing, if you want. That way you can get some sleep."

I can't help but be surprised at her offer. The east wing is where she and her mother have their rooms. For a second or two, I consider declining, but then a loud howl from one of her crew convinces me that if I don't, I might never get a moment of sleep again.

"Thank you. I appreciate that. I wouldn't be any good to you or anyone else if I'm always exhausted. I wouldn't want my protection of you to suffer because of that."

We sit silently looking at one another until suddenly she jumps up. "It's nothing. I'm still the same spoiled star you can't stand. This doesn't change that. Goodnight, Liam."

As I open my mouth to correct her, she hurries away before I can tell her I don't feel that about her, especially after she was so generous to give me a room away from her noisy crew. A twinge of guilt pinches at me that she truly believes I can't stand her.

I'm supposed to be her protector, the one person she can count on to keep her safe. What kind of bodyguard am I if she thinks I feel that way toward her?

CHAPTER SEVEN

 ia

I RUSH INTO AINSLEY'S ROOM AND SLAM THE DOOR behind me, pressing my back to it to make sure no one can follow me in here. I need to talk to someone, and out of all the people in this house, Ainsley is the one I can trust the most.

She looks up from whatever yoga pose she's in that makes her look like some kind of deformed pretzel and her eyebrows shoot up into her forehead, the only sign that she's surprised to see me. I usually let the crew settle in before I begin demanding anything of them.

"Sure, come on in. I guess I should be happy I decided to wear clothes for my evening stretch. You do remember I prefer to do this in the buff, right?" she says in that crabby voice she uses on me when I've overstepped my bounds.

I want to explain to her that this is my house, so there are no bounds, but I don't, preferring to keep her as an ally for what I have to say to her. "Sorry, but I've seen you naked dozens of times, Ains. Why aren't you doing your pretzel thing in the buff like always?"

She untwists herself while I wonder if Liam saw her naked and that's why my life coach is clothed for her nightly routine. Ainsley is a beautiful woman with a great body and beautiful long blond hair I would love to have, and unlike me, she isn't considered a spoiled pain in the ass.

Then again, her goat noises bothered him, so maybe he doesn't like her either.

"Earth to Mia. Come in, Mia."

Her voice tears me from my thoughts of whether or not Liam saw her naked, and I shake my head. "What?"

"I'm wondering why you're here. Is something wrong? Do you need help?" she asks.

"Liam couldn't sleep. He was wondering if you were birthing goats in here," I blurt out, not even sure why I'd tell her that.

The look she gives me tells me she isn't impressed with the new addition to my staff. "Liam. Hmmph. He looks like a Liam. Or a Henry. Something overbearing and bossy. Since when does what I do at bedtime concern anyone else?" she asks, returning to her cranky mood.

I quickly wave her question away. "Don't worry. I told him he could take one of the rooms on my side of the house, so he won't be bothering you."

Instead of making her happy, my comment seems to confuse her. At least that's the way it appears as she gives me a funny look like she doesn't understand a word I've said.

"Since when do you allow anyone to stay that close to you?"

Feeling exposed, like she can see right into my thoughts, I shrug and look away. "He's my personal bodyguard and head of my security team, so it's only right he's nearby. Right?"

"Right? Are you asking my permission to have the large, opinionated man who's got brooding down to a science close to you? If you are, I say no."

I can't help but smile. Ainsley always has a way of making me happy.

"Well, I'm not."

"Fine, but none of your other bodyguards have ever stayed on that side of the house. Speaking of that, where is Michael? Why isn't he here instead of Liam?"

The way she says Liam's name sounds like she already hates him. I don't think I'll bother to tell her the feeling is likely mutual.

"Michael's gone," I say, not wanting to explain anything more about him right now. "History. The past. Liam is my chief of security now, so that's that."

"Oookaaay."

The two of us stand in silence as I try to contain my emotions about Michael's leaving and my finding him with that girl. I don't want Ainsley to see me upset over it or she's going to want to talk about it, and the last thing I want to do is talk about that situation.

So I focus on the ugly pink color she chose to paint the walls in here instead, silently telling myself that while we're gone, the painters need to get in here and get rid of this color. Is it salmon? Chartreuse? No, that's green. Why couldn't she pick a nice delicate pink instead of this muddy shade of what used to be my favorite color?

"Is there something you want to talk about, Mia? You sounded okay on the phone the other day, but I'm assuming since you didn't tell me about Michael leaving and this new guy coming on board that you might want to talk."

Turning around, I force a smile and nod at her question. "You're the closest thing I have to a friend, Ainsley," I say in a low voice, suddenly ashamed at how few people I have in my life who I can talk to. "I need that now, so please, none of the life coach stuff when I tell you what's on my mind, okay?"

She gives me one of her sweet smiles I hope is genuine and takes a step toward me. Touching my hand, she says, "I am your friend, Mia. You can tell me anything. I won't tell a soul."

Unsure how to approach what I'm thinking about because I don't know what I'm feeling at this moment, I simply repeat the word Liam used and ask, "Do you think I'm gorgeous?"

"Yes. Why?" Ainsley asks, sitting down on her bed.

"Even with this purple mess still in my hair?" I ask, nervously tugging on the ends near my nape.

"Yes. Again, why?"

"Do you think someone like me could ever find love?" I ask, looking down into her light green eyes to see the truth in case she lies because she feels like she has to.

"Yes, and hoping the third time's a charm, why?"

"I just wanted to know. That's it."

Her eyes fill with sadness, and she asks, "Is this about Michael? Is that what this is all about?"

Suddenly, I can't stop the tears from coming. Burying my face in my hands, I let the misery I've felt since I saw him standing there with that girl in his apartment wash over me.

"I thought he cared about me. I thought that it didn't matter that we weren't sleeping together because he loved me. I thought we were soulmates, Ains. I really thought he cared about me. That he proved that someone could care about me and prove Jonny was full of it. I was so wrong. God, how could I have been so wrong?"

I feel Ainsley's arms envelop me, and I sink into her embrace. I've needed this from the second I realized Michael never cared like I thought he did.

"Oh, honey. He did. He cared about you. Whatever happened, he cared."

Shaking my head against her shoulder, I sob harder as I say, "No, he didn't. My mother fired him for getting me the hotel room, and he had a girl with him not two days later when I went to his place to talk to him. I thought after all that time we spent together after Jonny and I broke it off that he really cared about me. Not the me everyone else sees up on stage but the real me."

"I don't know why he did that, Mia. I just know he cared about you and he would have never let anyone hurt you."

"Then why was he with someone so soon? Days, Ains. Days. That's all it took to replace me. Days. It's been weeks and I'm still all alone," I ask as I lift my head off her shoulder and wipe the tears from my cheeks.

Ainsley gently takes me by the shoulders like she always does when she wants to make sure I'm listening to something she has to say. She looks straight into my eyes and shakes her head. "He wasn't good enough for you. He knew that, I bet. Don't give him another thought. You deserve the best this world can offer. Michael wasn't that. He knew it. Now you know it too."

I take a deep breath in and let it out in a rush, wishing all my sadness could go with it. "What if I'm not the best? What if I'm just some spoiled little girl who got lucky because of her voice?"

My life coach shakes her head again, but now she looks angry. "And just who told you that little bit of nonsense?"

"Jonny was the one who said that to me. Remember?"

Ainsley screws her face into a tight grimace. She never did like Jonny.

"Your ex was a horse's ass. Period. Full stop. You know better than to believe that guy. I know you do."

I hang my head and sigh. "Yeah. I guess."

"I thought maybe it was the new person in your life. I was really starting to dislike your new head of security if it was," she says, still scowling.

With a shrug, I try to tell her Liam isn't why I'm questioning everything about myself. Not really. "No. He didn't say anything. He's not like that. Well, maybe he is, but that's not why I'm asking you these things," I say as I sit down on the bed next to her.

"Then why? You're a beautiful person, Mia. Inside and out. I know you don't let everyone see that all the time, but that doesn't change the fact that you are. What's got you thinking that you're some spoiled little girl?"

I try to think of a way to explain what I'm feeling without bringing Liam into it. I don't need my life coach hating the only person I truly have to depend on when I leave this house. He's not the reason I'm doubting I'm worthy of having the best or ever finding love either.

Well, not the entire reason.

Wiping my tears away again, I shake my head. "I've been so lucky, Ains. So lucky. I wanted to sing, and the world has taken to my songs like I never dreamed it would. All the hard work has been worth it, so don't think I'm doubting that. It's just that at the end of the day, I sleep alone in my bed and it's been a long time since anyone even tried to be with me. The tabloids and social media are so sure I'm sleeping with half a dozen guys a week. If they only knew how it really was."

I stop before I say the one word that will get me crying again. I can't say it or I'll turn into a blubbering mess because it's true.

But before I can warn Ainsley not to say it either, she blurts it out. "How lonely it really is for someone like you?" she asks.

The tears come just as I knew they would, and this time I can't stop them. My body shudders as sobs wrack every inch of me because that single word is the truest expression of what my life is like.

Lonely.

I read in those rags they sell at the grocery stores that my mother insists on buying that I can have any man I want and I pick and choose who comes and goes from my bed. What a joke! My bed has me in it every night. That's it. Me and too many pillows because I went through that faze when I couldn't have enough of them on the bed.

But that's it. Mia and pillows. No hot men lining up to spend their nights with me. No picking and choosing. Just a single lonely woman wondering why if she's supposed to have her choice of everything in the world does she has nothing she wants.

Ainsley wraps her arms around my shoulders and squeezes me to her. "Oh, Mia, I'm sorry. I didn't mean to say the wrong thing. I know this life is hard for you. From the outside, you look like you have a picture perfect life with everything you want. Those horrible social media people make up all those stories about you being a terrible person or sleeping around, and every time I see one of them, I want to scream, so I can only imagine how you feel. Don't let them get you down. You aren't anything like those people say, and anyone who's close to you can attest to that."

"I wish."

That's not true, and she knows full well it isn't. My mother can't attest to that. She says what she knows the world has to hear to love me so the money can keep rolling in, but she doesn't believe a word that comes out of her mouth.

Her assistant and that person they hired to pretend to be me on social media don't believe any what Ainsley just said. They're like everyone else. They do what they have to in order to keep the world loving me, but they don't feel that way.

Liam doesn't think that way either. I know it. Every time he talks to me, I hear the disdain in his voice. I can tell even before my crew showed up that he regrets taking this assignment, as if protecting me is a chore and not something he truly wants to do.

"Honey, what's brought all of this on? Is it because we've all been away these past few weeks? You should have called me. I could have talked you down from this ledge so you didn't have to feel this way."

I push my hair off my face and wipe my tear-soaked cheeks for a third time. "I don't know, Ains. I just feel like in the past couple weeks everything I do is wrong. I don't want to feel this way, you know?"

Her pale green eyes fill with sympathy. My life coach has helped me weather all sorts of bouts of insecurity like this, and one of the most important parts of that is showing me she cares. Ainsley has no idea how much it means to see that in her eyes right now.

"Mia, I know you don't want to feel that way. Who would? We all want to feel like we're an important part of the world for ourselves and not for what we can do for other people. You're no different. What did I tell you the first day I met you? Do you remember?"

I nod and feel my mouth turn up into a smile like it always does when I think of that day. Ainsley had been referred to me by my ex-business manager, but by the time she got back from a vacation to see her family out in Colorado, George was gone, replaced by my mother, who didn't think I needed anything like a life coach. She tried to turn her away at the front gates, but Ains insisted, telling her that she wanted to meet me because she was a huge fan and could help my career. An hour later, I felt like I'd met my best friend in the world when she said those words to me I'll never forget.

"Everyone wants to be loved, Mia. Just because you look like you're loved more than other people doesn't mean you don't have the right to want to be loved when you're not in the limelight."

Those words come out like they're a mantra, something tattooed on my brain so I never forget that I deserve love like everyone else in the world. She smiles and nods as each syllable comes out loud and clear, just as she told me to say them that day.

"Exactly. You have every right to want to be loved in the way that makes you happy. Don't ever forget that."

And just as quickly as the good feelings come, they leave again when my fear that it will never happen surges inside me. "But what if no matter how much I want it, the love never happens?"

With a gentle smile, she shakes her head. "Impossible. You want it badly enough, it can't help but happen. Anyway, you're going to find someone who loves you in all the right ways. I know it. I knew it the first time I talked to you. You have such a great energy that people can't help but fall in love with you. Trust me. The man who's right for you is out there. You'll meet him. I have no doubt at all."

"Thank you, Ains. I needed to hear that tonight."

"That's what I'm here for, honey. It's literally my job to help you see how wonderful you are. Talk about a sweet gig," she says with a giggle.

"Well, thank you. Oh, by the way, I hate this pink in this room. It makes me feel like I'm in the middle of that medicine commercial."

Ainsley looks around at the ugly pink walls and lets out a heavy sigh. "It does sort of look like Pepto Bismol but with a dash of something gray. Maybe when we're gone the guys can paint it a nice pink."

"Exactly what I thought." Standing from the bed, I smile down at her. "I'll let you get back to your evening stretches. Thanks for helping me to see things clearly."

"Anytime, Mia."

When I get back to my side of the house, I wonder which room Liam took. I couldn't tell Ainsley how I'm starting to feel about him, and not just because she likely wouldn't approve, even if she does think I'm worthy of the kind of love I want.

I couldn't tell her because I'm not sure what I'm feeling. All I know is that when I saw him sitting by the pool tonight in those shorts and ratty old T-shirt, he looked like a different person and offering him a room near me on this side of the house seemed like the most natural thing to do.

Even if I've never once before with anyone who works for me even thought that for a second.

With one last glance down the hallway before I walk into my bedroom, I guess he's in the room farthest away from mine. It's a good choice since it has a fireplace that the other bedrooms don't. I can see him liking that, even though we rarely get weather cold enough to need that kind of heat here in Tampa.

Or maybe he chose that room because that's the farthest he can get away from me without being on the other side of the house where all the noise is.

CHAPTER EIGHT

iam

WHEN I WAKE UP AT FIVE TO GET MY WORKOUT IN, I'm thankful to hear nothing but silence. Never before in my life have I been so grateful to hear not a single noise. I know it won't last for long, so I hurry and get dressed so I can at least get something accomplished before the circus wakes up.

Then again, if they're like Mia, they might stay in bed until noon. I can only hope that's the case.

An hour later, my day has started out better than I could have expected after the arrival of the entourage. Nobody interrupted me while I was in the gym, and as I stroll around the pool area considering a swim before I get down to work, I see not a single soul.

This might just be okay. Sure, they were loud and obnoxious last night, but that doesn't mean they act like wild animals all the time. Maybe I was too hasty in my impression of them.

I enjoy some laps in the pool and then a good, hot shower afterward, regretting how easily I jumped to conclusions with Mia's crew. Toweling off, I gaze out my window and remind myself not to think so negatively. It's a habit I got into living with Wilder recently, but I need to break it now. Just because he's who he's always been doesn't mean everyone else is simply because I judge them on first impressions.

As I wrap the towel around my waist, I mull over what I have planned for today. I need to move the rest of my things to this new room on this side of the house, and then I need to speak to Andrea about who handles the security on Mia's tours since she's scheduled to go on the road in less than a month. I would have liked more time to prepare, but her mother's kept putting me off, saying we could talk the next day.

Of course, the next day came and went over and over, and still we haven't discussed plans I need to know in order to effectively keep her daughter protected.

But first, I need coffee. Caffeine then work.

The scent of that delicious blend from Sumatra that everyone here loves beckons me down the stairs. I have to admit, while much of this job is less than wonderful, the extra benefits of what I get to enjoy for meals makes up for a lot of it, and that coffee Andrea raves about is the best I've ever had, now that I asked the cook to make me my own pot that doesn't resemble hot beige water.

I pour myself a mug and splash in some milk and sugar, happy I'm the only person awake at this hour. It's barely seven in the morning, and I'm loving every moment of silence. Even the cook seems to have decided to leave me alone today.

An enormous room, the kitchen somehow feels cozy. It's probably the tan and brown granite the designer chose for the backsplash. Even with all the stainless-steel appliances and white cabinets, this room is warm and welcoming. It may be my favorite room in the house after my own.

Just as I lift the cup to my lips to enjoy that first sip of coffee for the day, my heart sinks as the sounds from last night begin again. Shaking my head, I sit down at one of the two islands in the center of the kitchen and silently mourn the loss of peace at the estate.

With every second that passes, the racket grows louder and louder. Someone's playing some kind of music that sounds like it wants to be salsa but whoever's playing the instruments have no clue about that kind of music. Or maybe it's that another one of the crew begins to play music in their room that clashes with the first person's, creating nothing but an auditory horror.

It doesn't matter because the end result is the same assault on the silence and my ears.

Before I can finish my coffee, all six of them flood into the kitchen and begin to make breakfast for themselves. Each person talks over the others, and I'm sure no one is actually listening to anyone but themselves. They laugh, presumably at their own jokes since they can't hear anything else, and in a matter of minutes, I feel like I'm trapped in the world's busiest beehive, except this one involves pancakes and something the personal trainer brings out of the refrigerator that smells like feet.

None of them acknowledge my presence, which is fine, but it's almost like they insist on pretending they're the only people in the house. Since Mia's not up yet, I have to wonder why none of them are worried they might wake her.

I consider asking, but I can't seem to get the words to form as I watch in dismay while they demolish the kitchen that had been clean before they arrived just a few minutes ago. One of the women, the one I think might be that ridiculous life coach who was making goat noises last night, gives me a sideways glance that may be a glare, but that's about all the acknowledgement they afford me as they buzz around like the most annoying bugs ever to exist.

When I stand up to set my dirty coffee mug on the counter, I have to push my way through the trainer and his stinky breakfast and one of the two hair stylists to get even near to the sink. The woman huffs her irritation that I've interrupted whatever the hell she's doing with an onion bagel and the jar of peanut butter she's dunking it into, but I ignore her and deposit my mug where Andrea told me we put the dirty dishes.

"You know, you could wash that," one of the women says behind me. "It's not like it's that hard."

Something snaps inside me, and I whip around to see five women and Mitchell staring at me with looks of disgust on each of their faces. So they're disgusted with me? Well, they have no idea how much I already can't stand them. Forget all that nonsense about jumping to conclusions. I was right with my first impression of all of them. They're rude, presumptuous, and whatever the fuck the woman next to the sink is doing with the damn peanut butter is downright gross.

"You know what's not that hard? Remembering that the world doesn't revolve around you? Oh, and if you think I'm talking to someone other than you, you're wrong. You burst into the house last night like you own the place, waking everyone up with your bullshit, and guess what? None of it is funny or charming or whatever the hell you think you are. Nope. Just irritating. Some of us actually have jobs here that involve something other than focusing on our own needs, so why don't you get the hell out of the way so we can do them?"

I think the last time I had that many people staring at me with such anger was when Cash, Cade, Alex, Wilder, and I came home from jail and we had to face all of our parents at once. At least they had some feeling of affection for me. These six look like they'd hog-tie me and roast me over a fire if any of them were strong enough to take me.

In the silence, their hatred for me comes through loud and clear, so I leave without having a single thing for breakfast, just another reason I can't stand any Mia's crew. On my way upstairs, Andrea catches me looking all happy, like any of what's happening around us is normal.

"Good morning, Liam. Did you have breakfast already?" she asks in a chipper voice.

"No," I grunt out, still fuming from all those people ruining yet another day in my life.

"I'm sure Cecelia would be happy to make you anything you want. I know you don't tend to eat like we do, but she's a fantastic cook. We love having her working here for us."

Something about the way she says that stops me cold, and I turn around and march back down the stairs to ask her about who all works here and why we all need to live here. The noise in the kitchen returns as each of those selfish people begins talking again, no doubt ignoring everyone else in the room once more.

I point toward where they babble on and on and shake my head. "What is this? How can people live like that? They show up last night making enough noise to wake the dead, and this morning they get up and it's the same decibel level of nonsense. How long will this continue?"

Andrea glances toward the kitchen and then smiles at me. "Oh, they're here until Mia goes out on tour. This is her routine when she's getting ready to go on the road. Everyone lives with her here and they spend every waking moment together getting in synch."

The way she explains it makes it seem perfectly normal that a circus has moved into Mia's house. Sure.

Who doesn't have a hoard of obnoxious people storming in at midnight and then taking over?

Then I realize the worst part of this all. "They don't go until she does, and they'll be around all the time when she's out on tour?" I ask in dread as images of chaos fill my mind.

I'll never have another peaceful moment on this job. Fuck.

Nodding her head enthusiastically, Andrea answers, "Oh, yeah. They're Mia's people. She can't do a tour without them. She'd be lost."

I wish they'd get lost. Permanently.

"Okay. Thanks. It might be a good idea for you to inform me ahead of time of any people joining the household, Andrea. My job is to protect your daughter. It's ten times more difficult when I don't know the circumstances of who's living here."

Patting me on the shoulder, she smiles. "Next time. I didn't think of it this time because I'm used to them all. They're so full of life. I love how they make Mia feel."

Like the Mad Hatter?

I don't say that, but instead take advantage of having Andrea here to ask her about the security on the tour. She explains that it's hired out through her management company to local officials and contractors. Why she couldn't tell me that the first time I asked her about this and every time since I have no idea.

"Then I'm going to need a full list of every agency and contractor involved and ASAP. I need to coordinate with each group in every city on the tour."

I take a step to walk back upstairs, but Andrea's look of confusion stops me. "Is there something wrong?"

She shakes her head, but it's obvious she has some issue with what I've just requested. "No. It's just that we've never done it like that."

The noise in the kitchen suddenly grows loud enough again that my head starts pounding. "Never done what like that? I'm sure Michael as the head of her protective unit dealt with each group on the tour stops, didn't he?"

"No. I've always been the one who's handled things. The businesses we use are very professional and have never failed to keep Mia safe."

Is this woman serious?

"So what did Michael do when Mia went out on the road?" I ask in stunned amazement that one of the biggest stars in the world has had such lax protection.

Andrea shrugs. "He went with her, of course."

"To do what, exactly? See the sights? Take a vacation? What was he doing if he wasn't making sure everything was in place with the security for Mia?"

"He was always nearby. It's not like he left her alone or hung out at the hotel. I don't want you thinking that's how things were because they weren't. I'm just not sure why you need to coordinate with every place that provides security for the shows."

I lean down so I'm in Andrea's face and answer her. "So no crazy maniacs get close to your daughter.

She's one of the most known people on the planet, Andrea. You don't think there are people who want to get to her? Consider yourself lucky that she didn't get hurt because of the way you people have been handling security up to this point. Christ, you should consider yourself lucky that someone didn't just pluck her up and take her prisoner. She's a superstar. People get obsessed with women like Mia. So get me that list and get it to me today so I can start to contact each of these people and make sure no one gets to your daughter who isn't cleared to be near her."

As I storm up the stairs, I can't decide if Mia's mother is simply negligent or actually someone who might want to see her daughter get hurt. Maybe not consciously, but damnit she has a funny way of showing she wants to protect her. She gets Jonah to convince me to take this job, supposedly because I'm perfect for it, and then she just thinks things are going to stay status quo when basically all her last head of security did was lounge around like one of Mia's friends on an extended sleepover.

I should have known this assignment would be a nightmare just by how much he was willing to pay me to take it. All the warning signs were there, but I ignored them because my mother convinced me of something that isn't remotely close to being true.

Thankfully, within an hour, Andrea emails me the list of each contractor and security personnel in the cities Mia's scheduled to perform in, but it only takes a few calls for me to realize I need more men working directly with me if this tour is going to be as safe and secure as I want it to be. The locals Andrea has always worked with are good, but they aren't good enough for one of the world's biggest stars.

I find Andrea in her office down on the first floor near the living room and have to marvel at the quiet that's come over the house. The entourage must have all gone out for the day. Thank God for small favors.

As I walk in to sit down so we can discuss how to get the men I need here as quickly as possible, she smiles and asks, "You got my email? I made sure to send it as soon as I got in here this morning."

"I did. That's what I'm here about. I need more men, so I'm going to contact Jonah at VIP today and get things moving so they can get up to speed before the tour starts. I don't want to work with anyone who isn't fully on board when things get going. I think four should do it."

Her smile quickly disappears, and she shakes her head as worry settles into her expression. "Oh, Mia isn't going to like that."

"Well, I'll explain it to her. She'll see I'm right," I say as I stand to leave, already tired after only half a day awake.

"You're going to have to do more than that. Only Mia can approve your request. I may handle things involving security, but I technically stepped over the line when I got rid of Michael. If you want more men, you need to get her to agree."

"Okay. I'll handle that now because I don't want any of us to be caught flat-footed when the tour begins," I say as I head out to find Mia.

After our talk last night, I don't anticipate any problems with my request. The woman gave me a room on her side of the house when she saw how noisy her crew was. This will be nothing compared to that.

I spy her out near the pool with the six of them and walk out there to get things moving on this project. All of them are sprawled out on chaise lounges in bikinis, all except Mitchell who somehow thought a white Speedo was a good choice for today. Stifling my need to chuckle at how idiotic he looks lying there, I stop beside Mia and look down at her.

It occurs to me that I've never seen her in a bathing suit in all the time I've lived and worked here. I had no idea she had such a great body. She never works out, so it must be natural.

At least that's what it looks like in her black string bikini.

"I need to speak to you for a few minutes. Nothing big, but it needs to be handled today," I say when she doesn't open her eyes to acknowledge my presence.

She looks up at me and waves her hand to dismiss me. "Later. We're busy."

Yet another time today I'm stunned. I look around at the group of them to see they're doing nothing but lying in the sun. She can do that anytime. Hell, as soon as she hears me out and gives me the green light for more guys, she can go back to doing nothing.

"No. Now."

Those two words get all eyes on me, and I find the six of her crew staring daggers at me. Mia sits up, almost as if she can't believe I said no, and shakes her head. "Are you deaf? I said we're busy."

I look down into her dark eyes flashing rage and shake my head at her. "And I said I need to talk to you. Now."

Grabbing her white cover up, she rips it off the back of the chaise lounge and storms away without a word, leaving me with the people who started my day off like shit glaring up at me like I'm some kind of fucking villain because I need to do my job. I follow her inside and find her fuming in the living room, pacing back and forth, her bare feet making a slapping sound with each angry step on the tile.

Before I can speak, Andrea walks into the room from her office and only takes a second to size up the situation. She probably feels the anger coming off both of us because as soon as she takes two steps toward us, she spins around and hurries back out. I stand there in amazement that everyone tolerates this nonsense from Mia. How the hell does anything get done around here?

"I heard what you said to my friends this morning. I should make you apologize," Mia snaps on one of her passes by me.

"For what? Informing them of the fact that they're the most self-centered people I've ever met? I won't apologize for telling the truth. Now what I wanted to talk to you about was security."

She stops in front of me and holds her hand up in front of my face. "I didn't finish what I wanted to say, so I'm not interested in what you have to say yet."

I tilt my head left and right, hoping to crack my neck and possibly ease the tension headache that's making me feel like the top of my skull is about to blow off. "Mia, I won't apologize to them, but if I upset you, then I'm sorry. Now I need to talk about security for your tour."

"Talk to my mother. She handles all of that. Now if you're done intruding on my meditation time, I'm going to go back and hope to find my center again."

Mia moves to walk around me, but I step in front of her, blocking her path. "Not yet. I need four more men to work directly with me while you're on tour. The locals your mother has aren't good enough. She says I need your okay, so as soon as you give it, we can be done."

Her face lights up in shock. "Four more? Four more men like you? No way!"

"You're damn lucky nothing's happened to you so far, Mia. The security situation your mother and those local people at each tour stop have going is lax, to say the least. I need men working directly for me to make sure you're safe."

Taking a step closer to me, she stops just before her cover up touches my arm and shakes her head. "No. I already feel like I'm trapped in this house. Four more of you and I'll feel like a prisoner of war. No way."

"I can't do my job without those four men. If you can't agree to this, then I'll have to resign. VIP send someone to replace me by tomorrow, I'm sure. Your choice, Mia."

When I look down into her dark eyes, I see the idea of my leaving bothers her. She's probably worried that someone new would be even more of a hardass than I am.

"Two, but no more."

I shake my head, unwilling to bargain on this point. "Four or I go. Your choice."

She stares up at me with rage in her eyes, but there's something else there I see now too. I can understand why so many men think she's one of the most beautiful women in the world. The way she can infuriate a person while at the same time looking so breakable like she needs him to protect her from the harshness of the world is very seductive.

That's nothing I can let in, though. Getting involved in any way with a client is always a mistake.

Still, I can't deny she has an effect on me.

CHAPTER NINE

ia

HE'S CLOSE ENOUGH THAT I FEEL THE HEAT COMING off his body. I've never felt that from anyone in my entire life. Is it because he's so much bigger than me, or was he working out before he came to talk to me out at the pool?

I glance down and notice he's wearing jeans, so he couldn't have been at the gym. Is he always this hot? Like literally hot?

Maybe if he didn't insist on wearing a dress shirt in eighty-degree weather. That would explain why he's so hot. I can't stop myself from inhaling, curious to know if he's sweating. It's weird, but this man intrigues me. One minute he has nothing but utter contempt for everything I am, yet the next minute he's here telling me he needs more people to make sure I'm safe.

"Tell me why you need four more of you. Michael never needed anyone else. He thought the locals, as you call them, were fine."

Liam rolls his eyes and smiles in that way that tells me he's about to insult someone. I've only been around him for a few weeks, but I already know when he's about to lay some verbal smackdown on someone.

"Michael was a moron when it came to keeping you safe. I told your mother this and I'll tell you. You're damn lucky no one yanked you off the street and took you home to make you his personal Mia doll. With the security as careless as it's been in the past, I can't believe you're still here to go out on tour at all."

The way he says that, so intense and in that deep voice of his, frightens me. Taking a step back, I try not to be freaked out, but I can't stop myself. I feel vulnerable, something I hate.

"Really? It was that bad? Why would my mother do that?"

Liam frowns, making his very attractive face look even more serious than it usually does. "Because she's not a security specialist. For what it's worth, either was Michael. I am, though, and I'm telling you I can't stay as your head of security with such slipshod protection surrounding you."

Every word out of his mouth sounds more terrifying than the last, and I feel myself start to become overwhelmed by fear. I need to fight the urge to hide in my shell and never come out again, though. I've learned that from Ainsley.

"Liam, I can't live like I'm some caged animal.

Even out on tour, I need to feel normal. I can't perform if I'm freaked out with people hovering over me like I'm always in danger."

"You won't have to be."

He says that with such certainty that I want to believe him. "You say that, but four more guards means exactly that. I'll be trapped."

Liam's face turns hard for a moment, and I brace for him to fight me more on this. He doesn't, though, pleasantly surprising me.

In a soft voice that might be even sexier than his usual deep voice, he says, "Mia, my one and only job is to protect you. That's it. That's all I'm trying to do."

I let out a heavy sigh and shake my head. "Why does it have to feel so oppressive?"

Still in that soft tone, he answers, "I don't want it to feel like that. I promise we'll be invisible. You'll probably forget we're even around."

I look up to see a kind expression on his face. "I doubt that."

"I'll do everything in my power to make sure you don't know we're around. I promise."

When I stare into his blue eyes, I secretly hope I won't forget he's around. I like knowing he's nearby. He drives me nuts and every person in my crew hates him, but I've grown to like Liam being in my life. I didn't know how much I needed to truly feel safe until he came along.

"I just don't want to feel like a prisoner, Liam. That's all."

"And I don't want to feel like your jailer."

Not able or even interested in fighting him on this anymore, I nod and let out a sigh of surrender. "As long as I don't have the four of them hanging around constantly."

"You won't."

"I mean, you being around is enough. Four more of you and I think I might go crazy," I say with a smile.

He understands I'm attempting to be nice and smiles back. "So you're okay with me being around? I can only imagine how much your entourage hates that."

"A lot, but you aren't working for them. You're working for me, and as long as you agree that I do what I want, when I want, we'll be fine."

Suddenly, all the softness and happiness in him fades away, leaving that hard man I met the first day he came here. The intensity in his gaze frightens me now as he looks down into my eyes like he's trying to make me understand something I refuse to.

But then he begins to speak, and I know he's still the man I've grown to enjoy having around me.

"Mia, I would lay down my life if it meant you were safe. If that's a problem, maybe you should tell me now so I can resign and VIP can provide you with another head of security. But if you want to be sure you're safe, then I need to do my job and that may mean you don't get to do what you want whenever you want."

For the second time in this conversation, he's mentioned resigning, and both times, my chest tightened at the mere words. I don't know why, but I hate the thought of him leaving and not being in my life anymore. I don't understand it since we barely know each other, but the pain in my chest tells me I want him to stay.

Even more, Michael never made me feel this safe, and never once did he say he'd die for me.

So I quietly relent and give Liam what he wants. "I can live with that. And the four more guys."

That makes him smile, and for a moment, I get lost in how sexy he looks when he gets what he wants. "I'll start working on that this afternoon so we're ready for when the tour kicks off next month."

"Thank you. For everything," I say, wishing I had more to discuss with him as he moves to walk away.

I can't think of anything, so he keeps moving toward the hallway, looking back at me as he says, "You're welcome, but there's no need to thank me. It's my job."

With every step, he gets farther away, and I wish I had any reason to stop him. I know it's stupid, but something about the way he said it's just his job hurt my feelings.

That's silly, though. It is his job to protect me. He was just stating the obvious.

Nothing would never work between the two of us anyway, so I need to stop thinking about how sexy he is when he smiles and how gorgeous his blue eyes are when he's trying to convince me to do something I don't want to do. He's not my type.

The Liams of the world are too serious for the

Mias of the world. He's all rules and regulations, and I need to run free. Or at least I need to feel like I'm not being chained to the floor every second of the day. He spends his time worrying about security, and all I want to do is have fun and live my life.

No, we would never work out. Still, I can't deny I like him.

"What did Mr. Tight Ass want?"

I turn to see Ainsley standing next to me watching Liam walk away down the hall. "See anything you like there, Ains?"

Her cheeks instantly grow red, and she gives me a scowl. "Him? Are you kidding? His chi and my chi would not work together. The man has no yin in him. He insists on constantly conquering every situation he encounters. He's like yang overload."

Liam disappears out the door to the gardens as I get my last look at him and Ainsley's complaints about him filter through my brain. "He said he'd die for me. Michael never said that. No one has ever said that."

"He's a bodyguard, Mia. It's sort of in the job description. I'm sure they're paying him a king's ransom to keep you safe. I wouldn't put too much stock in him saying he'd die for you. That's just all that yang."

I smile and nod, knowing she's right. "Yeah, sure. I know. It did feel nice to hear, though. I mean, who wouldn't like to know there's someone who would lay down their life to protect you?"

"Mia, that guy doesn't have an ounce of the feminine in him. It's like he's a total Alpha. Just being around him takes all the happiness out of me. I don't know how you do it."

Shrugging, I smile, but not too big so she can see how much I like spending time around Liam. "I don't know. I think of him like a challenge."

Unimpressed, she makes a face that looks like she just ate something gross. "Sure, but does he ever not come into a room like he's Captain America? Maybe if he didn't give off the vibe that he hated everyone, including you, ninety percent of the time, I could see someone finding him sort of attractive."

"He doesn't hate you," I say before turning to head back outside to the pool. "Just your goat noises."

I chuckle when I hear her huff in disgust behind me. "They are not goat noises. You know, I think you and that guy spent too much time alone without me and the rest of the crew here to act as a buffer. He's already rubbing off on you. You never thought my evening stretches sounded like goat noises before he said that."

She's right, but I won't tell her that. I don't want her to hate Liam, especially now that I know I definitely don't hate him.

"I was only kidding, Ains. Let's go back outside and see if I can slough off all of his yang and make you happy."

Next to me, she grumbles, "That's going to take an old priest and a young priest, at the very least. Talk about yang overload. Someone should cut back on his energy drinks. I think he's got too much testosterone coursing through his system."

I wrap my arm around her shoulders and squeeze her to me. "I love you, Ains. You never fail to make me smile."

That makes her happy, so she gives up her complaining about the other person who always seems to have a way to make me smile. I won't tell her about that, though.

CHAPTER TEN

iam

MY EYES FLY OPEN AT THE SOUND OF SOMEONE yelping, or maybe that's the life coach with her goat birthing noises. I scrub the sleep from my face and look around. Where am I? Nothing looks familiar.

Oh, right. I switched rooms a couple nights ago. Nothing like waking up to the sound of some animal in agony to confuse a guy.

I slowly come to my senses and realize it's Mia's entourage making all the noise. Because of course it is. I yearn for the days before they arrived. I truly do.

As I grumble to myself about how selfish these people are, I look out the window and see the sun isn't even up yet. God, what time is it?

Grabbing my phone, I see 4:40 in big white numbers across the screen. Did I somehow sleep through an entire night of them partying, or has something else kept them up all night? It has to be that they haven't gone to bed yet because these are not the type of people to wake up early.

The noise continues, and I figure out it's not in the west wing. Did they decide to take over the entire house? How does Mia live like this? She didn't stay up all night before they got here.

I roll out of bed and grab a pair of gray sweatpants and a white T-shirt from the dresser that's on the opposite side of the room from where it used to be. Still sort of groggy, I don't bother putting shoes on, instead grabbing my slides. If these people want a professionally dressed me, then they shouldn't wake me up before five in the morning.

My head begins to throb with every step down toward the main living area where the six people I hate the most in the world have gathered to make a commotion for some reason. I see Andrea dressed in a white robe pacing back and forth across the living room and wonder if there's been bad news.

"What's going on?" I ask, still not fully awake and needing coffee, but curious.

Andrea stops her path across the room a few feet from where I stand and wrings her hands. I notice she looks genuinely worried too.

"Mia's stalker's back."

Stalker? How the fuck is it that the man in charge of protecting Mia hasn't heard about this goddamned stalker before this? I swear to God these people want to see her hurt.

Suddenly wide awake, I ask, "Back? What do you mean?"

I think if she gives me some nonsensical answer like she does so often when she answers my questions that I'm going to blow a gasket this time. Thankfully, this morning, Andrea seems to be willing to tell all, which saves me from having to show yet again that I have no patience for these people.

"He's been silent for over a year. Everyone thought that he had just given up. Some of us, including the police, thought that maybe he died. I'd hoped he'd never return, but with her tour coming up, I guess we shouldn't be surprised," she says before she turns and resumes her pacing back toward the entrance to the hallway.

"Uh, did any of you even for a moment consider the idea of telling me about this stalker?" I ask, not even trying to hide my frustration at being kept in the dark about this.

Andrea shrugs as she turns around to come back toward me. "We didn't think it was worth mentioning. I mean, he's been gone for over a year. Stalkers usually don't disappear for that long without something bad happening to them, right?"

"Well, you should have told me anyway. How the hell am I supposed to keep Mia safe when I don't know all the dangers that may be lurking out there? I need you to tell me everything you know about this stalker. I'm serious, Andrea. Leave nothing out."

She stops in front of me again and sighs. "Okay. As I said, he's been gone for over a year. Every other time, he would start sending her letters just about a month before she went out on tour. The last time he didn't, so I thought we were in the clear. But a few hours ago, one of the letters arrived."

I hold up my hand to stop her before she goes any further. "How? It's the middle of the night. The post office certainly didn't deliver it after midnight, and I'm doubting Fed Ex or UPS did either. So how did it get here? Who found it and where?"

Andrea flails her arms in front of her face like she's trying to shoo away a bug and begins to cry. "I found it. It came in yesterday's mail, but I didn't get to look at everything that was delivered until late last night. I found it in the middle of the stack, the same white envelope with a heart drawn where the return address should be. I swear, Liam, my blood ran cold when I saw that because that's what the stalker always put on the envelopes before."

Okay, so it did come by mail. That's good. We can probably find out something from the post office if we have the envelope.

"What did you do with it?" I ask, certain she didn't call the police. If anything, Andrea would have called someone in the media first.

"I talked to her crew about it and we agreed I should give it to Mia, like I always do. She has it up in her room. She won't come out. She's a nervous wreck. Every time before, the letters would start coming and she'd fall apart right before the tour. She's like that now too. She keeps saying, 'He's come back' over and over. We're all beside ourselves with worry."

"Okay. I'm going to go up to talk to Mia. You calm these people down. All this hysteria isn't going to do your daughter any good. If they keep this up, she's never going to be in any shape to go out on tour, so get them out of here if they can't relax."

Andrea's mouth drops open in shock. "What do you mean she won't be able to go out on tour? She has to. Three weeks from now, the first show is scheduled for the pavilion right here in Tampa. She can't miss the show that kicks off the tour."

"Then calm down her entourage. How can anyone expect her to perform with all this madness surrounding her?" I say as I start back up the stairs to go speak to Mia.

"This is always how they are, Liam. Mia's used to it."

Stopping on the staircase, I glare down at her and snap, "Then she's been used to being mistreated. Now stop those goddamned people from making all that noise and let me do my job!"

I storm away, already sick and tired of everyone excusing the behavior of the crew. How any of those people, especially her supposed life coach, help Mia accomplish anything is beyond me. They've brought nothing but chaos since they arrived, well, except for those moments out near the pool where they were all naval gazing about something or another when I interrupted them.

And why the hell would her mother give her a letter from a goddamned stalker before letting me examine it first? I swear that woman is as bad as Mia's ridiculous crew. They thrive on turmoil, but what good did she think would come from throwing her daughter into emotional upheaval?

Gently, I knock on Mia's door, and she barks, "Go away!"

"Mia, it's Liam. I need to talk to you."

I get nothing but silence in response, so I repeat myself and add, "I can help with this. I just need you to open the door and let me."

Still silence. I can understand her fear and even anger at having to deal with this right before she leaves the safety of her home for the road, but I can't do anything for her if she doesn't let me in.

Finally, after a few minutes of waiting, she opens the door only a crack and looks up at me. Her eyes are red, and it looks like she's been crying.

"You're still here. People usually get the hint when I go silent on them. Why didn't you leave?" she asks, clearly confused that someone finally either stood their ground or cared enough to bother to wait.

"Since your entourage woke me up in the middle of the night and I'm wide awake now, I figured I'd hang out. Can I come in?"

Mia steps back and opens the door wide for me to walk in, saying as I pass, "You wake up every day at five, Liam. It's not like my people woke you up that much earlier than you usually get up."

Surprised she knows my schedule, I smile as she shuts the door and walks over to flop down on the king size bed in the middle of the room. "Well, those fifteen minutes are precious."

She rolls her eyes and covers them with her arm. "I know what you're going to say, and you didn't have to bother coming up here to say it."

"What's that?" I ask as I glance around her room with its pale pink walls.

"That the police will find this guy and it will all be okay. Well, they won't and it won't, so if that's all you have to say, just go now and save us both the trouble."

"That's not what I came up here to say."

For a long moment, she doesn't respond, but then she lowers her arm and sits up to look at me. "Really? That's what Michael usually told me."

"And I told you Michael was a moron. You don't have to be afraid. I won't let anyone harm you. I promise. I just need to see the letter."

Mia stares at me with a blank look for a few seconds and then asks, "Is that what you wear to bed? Who wears gray sweatpants to bed? By the way, don't let Mitchell see you in them or you're going to have your own personal stalker living less than a hundred yards away from you."

I don't try to stifle my laughter at what I think is her attempt at being cute. "I'll keep that in mind, and no, I don't wear these to bed. Now where's the letter?"

Pointing at the dresser on the other side of the room, she says, "Same as always. I guess there's something comforting in the fact that he never changes."

The first thing I notice is the envelope has no return address and a red heart outline drawn on the top left-hand corner instead, just as Andrea had described. What it does have is what every letter that's been through the post office must have—a barcode that will tell us where it was mailed from, hopefully, or at least what post office handled the letter.

Turning around, I look down at Mia and motion toward the bed. "Mind if I take a seat."

"Mi cama es tu cama."

As I sit down next to her, I ask, "Do you speak Spanish fluently?"

"No. I know the basics. In fact, I wouldn't be surprised if I screwed some of that up. I learned from the maid my mother brought in when I was thirteen. My tutors couldn't get me to learn anything in Spanish, and trust me, they tried, but Isobel had a natural ability to teach me. I can read it much better than I can speak it."

Interesting. I hadn't pegged Mia for someone who'd take an interest in anything like speaking a foreign language.

"Okay. Here's the good news. See these little lines on the bottom of the envelope? That's a bar code. I'll be able to find out at least where this letter was before it came here, and hopefully, that will give us some clue."

"Really? Then why didn't the cops ever find that out all the other times I got a letter."

"No idea. Maybe they didn't get the envelope?" I ask, wondering why they wouldn't have been able to at least learn that detail.

Mia rolls her eyes again. "That would explain it. My mother probably threw it out and only handed them the letter itself. Speaking of which, it's the same as always. Again, some comfort in the status quo, I guess."

While I read over the actual letter, I mumble, "I guess."

Her stalker doesn't say much. The letter in its entirety is comprised of only two actual sentences. Your mine and always will be Mia. I will see you soon.

Not exactly Shakespeare.

"Well, I'm guessing your stalker is a male and young. The misspelled you're as your gives that away. Not that there aren't women who would misspell that, but my money is on a man. Not too old, though."

I glance over and see Mia smiling. "At least it's not some creepy old dude with a bald head and missing teeth."

Shaking my head, I chuckle. "I can't say if he's a toothless wonder or if he has summer teeth. I'm just saying it's a male."

She tilts her head to the side a little and looks at me with confusion in her eyes. "Summer teeth?"

"Yeah. Summer there and some are not. Summer teeth."

For the first time, possibly since I arrived at her home, I see her truly laugh, like she thinks my joke is genuinely funny. It's great to see her happy like this too. It makes her even more beautiful.

"You are too funny, Liam. Summer teeth. I like that. So amaze me and explain why you think this person is young, which by the way, I agree with but only because my fans tend to be under forty."

Remembering what I learned when I was guarding the senator last year and he had a stalker, I point to the misspelled your that begins this letter. "Older people aren't used to spellcheck as much as younger people, so they tend to spell better. Even when they're threatening people, they tend to spell things right." I stop and see her nodding before I add, "That and the demographics of the people who enjoy your music tend to be younger."

"So I have a young male stalker. Not really shocking, but I still hate it."

"This happens almost every time you're about to go out on tour?" I ask, wondering if Andrea knew more than she was telling me before.

"He didn't send anything last year, but all the times before that, yeah. And then I wait for another one that never comes and I spend all my time looking around corners assuming a stalker is waiting to grab me. It makes me hate who I am every time."

"Well, not this time."

"Really?" she asks in a tone of utter disbelief.

"Yeah. That's not how we're playing this game. I'm here this time, so no worrying about someone waiting for you because if he's around, I'll find him first."

Mia gets a sheepish look on her face and hangs her head. "You probably think I'm stupid right now. Just yesterday, I gave you a hard time about hiring more men. You probably feel pretty vindicated."

"This isn't a competition between us to see who's right. I'm here to keep you safe. That's all I care about."

Instantly, her entire demeanor changes, and she jumps up from the bed. "I don't want to talk about this. Go."

Confused, I stand to leave, not knowing what made her change from that happy and relaxed woman to this one that appears to be coming apart at the seams. As she stands in front of me looking like she's about to burst into tears, I try to think of something to say to make that happier version of her come back.

"Okay. I'll call the cops and report this. They're going to want to talk to you, but I'll be there with you, if you want."

Anger explodes out of her. "No! No cops! I told them the first two times he sent me a letter, and they did nothing. They don't care about stalkers until they hurt someone. I don't want to have to deal with them. Bring them in when he finally gets to me."

Before I can say a word to let her know I won't let anyone get to her, she collapses onto the bed and sobs into her hands. It's heartbreaking to stand here and watch her fall apart. I don't know if I should leave and tell one of her crew to come up here for her or if I should stay.

I sit down next to her, not sure if she'll begin yelling again or something worse, but all she does is cry. When she stops, we sit in silence for a long time. I don't know what to say. At this moment, I wish I was one of those men who knows how to cheer someone up, but I'm not funny or kind enough. I never have been.

Finally, she softly says, "I bet you're regretting taking this job, aren't you?"

As much as I have hated many things about this assignment, at this very moment, I don't hate it, so I answer truthfully, "No. No regret at all."

Maybe one. I wish I knew how to show others I care.

 ia

Drying my eyes, I look over at Liam, surprised he isn't regretting the fact that he said yes to working for me. "Really?"

"This is my job. It's who I am. It's what I'm good at. It's all I've ever been good at going back to when I was a kid. Protecting people. Back then, it was smaller kids being picked on by bigger kids who thought they could push others around. Now it's this. So I'd never regret this or any job where I can do what comes naturally to me."

"Even after the crew showed up?"

He hesitates for a moment and then shakes his head. "Even then."

"Your girlfriend or wife is a lucky woman."

Liam smiles and shakes his head again. "No wife or girlfriend."

Maybe Mitchell was right when he claimed last night Liam would be his by tour's end. "Are you gay?"

A slow smile lifts the corners of his very appealing mouth. "No. I just don't have anyone in my life right now."

"I see. You probably had a terrible relationship with your mother growing up and think all women are a hassle. I can definitely see you as one of those guys," I say, more than a little disappointed he's that type of man.

But he laughs at my characterization of him, which makes me smile. "Not at all. I love my mother. She's an incredible woman and one of my biggest fans. I have no deep-seated problems with women. Just haven't found anyone I want to be serious with, especially since I'm often away from home."

Happy to hear he isn't some troubled guy with mommy issues, I probe a little more about his life, curious about the man who didn't leave when I didn't open the door before and didn't leave when I fell apart a minute ago.

"I bet she's tall like you with legs that go on forever and dark hair with blue eyes that make her look exotic, right?" I wonder aloud, imagining a woman similar to him.

That's probably why he hasn't found the woman he wants to be with. He's looking for someone like his mother.

I secretly sneak a glance down at my legs and

wonder if he'd consider them long. That's how they're usually described, but damn, if his mother is over six foot tall, her legs would be crazy long compared to mine.

Leaning off to the side, he takes his phone out of his sweatpants back pocket and brings up a picture of a tiny blond woman and a man who looks like the spitting image of him, just older. "The exact opposite, actually. Not tall. No dark hair. Obviously, I take after my father."

He hands me his phone, and I study the picture for a few moments. Nice couple. Very attractive. Liam comes by his good genes naturally. His father looks so much like Liam that I might get them confused from a distance. His mother looks sweet, like the kind of mom everyone would like but she's still really cool.

Turning to look at Liam, I say, "You really do. Did you get any of your mother's genes? She's beautiful, by the way. Really beautiful."

As he takes his phone back, he shakes his head and smiles. "Nothing physical, but I think I get my need to want to protect people from her. She loves to take care of everyone around her."

"Did you have a nice childhood? She's gorgeous and I'm sure all your friends had huge crushes on her at one point or another, but did she bake cookies and cut the crust off your peanut butter and jelly sandwiches?" I ask, imagining him as a little boy and the apple of his mother's eye.

Laughing, he answers, "She did, but don't go thinking everything was perfect because it wasn't."

"I don't believe for a second that those two people and you weren't perfect together. No way. They have perfect written all over their faces."

Before I say the same thing about him, I stop myself. "Do you have any brothers and sisters?"

Liam nods, but I notice he doesn't smile when he answers, "One sister. Annalea is older than me. And one brother. Wilder is one year younger."

Now I understand. Liam's the middle child. That's why he doesn't think his childhood was perfect, even though he had a mom who baked cookies and cared enough to cut the crusts off his PB and J sandwiches.

"Ah, I get it. You're the middle child. It's the Jan Brady Syndrome. So which one was the bigger pain, the older sister or the younger brother?"

That brings a smile back to his face, and his eyebrows shoot up into his forehead to show his disbelief in my psychological diagnosis. "The Jan Brady Syndrome? What's that? I've never heard of anything like that."

Now it's my turn to look at him in disbelief. "The Brady Bunch? You know, the middle daughter was named Jan and she always felt left out. Marcia, Marcia, Marcia! Everything is always Marcia!"

By the look of complete confusion on his face, I see he has no idea about Jan Brady or her family's TV show from the seventies. What kind of person doesn't know about that?

"Well, now I know your childhood wasn't perfect because you've never seen the Brady Bunch. Dude, get some culture in your life."

With a chuckle, he says, "I'll see what I can do."

"So you didn't answer me. Which one caused you more grief, the older sister or younger brother?" I ask, pressing him for information even though I sense he doesn't want to talk about this subject.

He gives me an answer, though, so I have to give him credit for that.

"Younger brother. I'm curious. How did you know one of them gave me a hassle? Just a guess, or are you secretly a psychologist on the side?"

I point at his mouth and arch an eyebrow. "You didn't smile when you started talking about your brother and sister. Just a little tell."

Liam nods, clearly surprised I didn't just guess. "I'm impressed. Where did you learn to pick up on people's tells?"

"You learn to figure people out when you're the one they all depend on."

Even as I say those words, I feel like a complete fraud. I never figured out Jonny or Michael, so my track record on being able to figure people out is pretty damn sad.

He falls quiet for a long moment before he asks, "So no baking or cutting off the crust on your sandwiches from Andrea?"

"God no!" I say, knowing I'm betraying how bad she was with that kind of thing.

"Sorry."

Suddenly, I feel like he's pitying me, and I hate that. "It's okay. This is my life. It's always been this way. The only difference is back then I wasn't famous."

When he doesn't answer, I quickly shift the attention back to his family. "The way you feel about your mother sounds so great. I'm jealous, if you want to know the truth."

He doesn't say anything but stands to leave, disappointing me. "Don't make the mistake of thinking my family's perfect. Trust me. I should take you to meet them all. Fifteen minutes with them and you'll be thankful you're an only child."

"All of them? I thought you only had one brother and sister. Who would I be meeting in addition to them?"

"My family isn't just my mother and father with my sister and brother. My father's brothers and their wives and my cousins are always around too. It's like one big family, the Jackson and March clan. Then there's my grandmother who keeps us in line too."

As I listen to him describe this big extended family of his that he calls a clan, I can't help but be jealous. They sound incredible. And nothing like I've ever experienced in my life.

"That sounds great. You should be thankful you have all those people who care about you just because you're family, Liam."

The sadness in my voice comes through loud and clear, and for a second or two, I think about making a joke to hide it. It's no use, though. He senses it, and I see in his expression that look like he's pitying me again that I hate.

"I guess, but sometimes when you're in the middle of a family that big, it can be a lot. Sometimes you just want to be alone."

Shaking my head, I say the only thing I know to be true in my life. "You don't want to be alone. Trust me. It's not all it's cracked up to be."

Liam nods, but he doesn't understand. No one with a family the size of his could know how it feels to be truly alone.

CHAPTER TWELVE

ia

AFTER A DAY FILLED WITH PEOPLE WHO ACTED LIKE they were all walking on eggshells around me, I want to hear more about Liam and his big family that drives him crazy. I want to hear stories and imagine what it's like to be surrounded by people who love you no matter what, not because they have to or because of what you can do for them.

Halfway to his room, I remember it's nearly eleven o'clock. Liam gets up at five every morning to workout. He's probably asleep already.

I should just go back to my room, but it's like I crave hearing more about what I've never experienced in my life. So I take a deep breath and knock on his door, hoping he doesn't answer it looking like he just fell asleep and I woke him up.

My heart races as I wait there in the hallway of my own house. It's silly, but I'm anxiously eager to listen to him tell me about that family of his.

When the door opens, I see him standing in front of me in just a pair of shorts with a towel in his hand drying his wet hair. My eyes fill with the sight of muscles and tattoos. Who knew my chief of security had such a great body and was all tatted up? He always wears jeans and dress shirts or T-shirts that cover them.

"I'm sorry. Am I interrupting?" I ask, my gaze roaming over his washboard abs, muscular chest, and incredible biceps that have never looked this good with shirts over them.

He's got great legs too. I had no idea he was so built. He just always seemed big until this moment.

"Give me a minute and I'll get dressed. Come on in," he says with a hint of embarrassment in his voice before backing up to let me walk into his bedroom.

Staring at a skull tattoo at the top of his chest, I say, "Please don't feel like you have to because of me. You're in your part of the house. You should be comfortable."

Seriously. Don't cover up all of this gorgeousness because of me. I'd much rather you stay this way, although I'm not sure I'm going to be able to focus much on anything else if you do.

"It will only take a minute. Make yourself comfortable. I'll be right back," he says before grabbing jeans and a blue T-shirt and disappearing into the bathroom.

I glance around his room and notice it's neat. Like pristine neat. Where are his shoes? Does he really keep all his clothes in the dresser and closet? Is he always this tidy? Is it because he's not in his own home, or is this how he is? It looks like nobody stays in this room. Even the bed is perfect, as if the maid just came in and made it.

When he returns a minute later, he's fully dressed but I notice his T-shirt shows a little of the tattoo at the top of his right arm I saw that day when I was staring at him from my bedroom window. God, he's good-looking standing there with his hair damp and me remembering what he looked like before he put on clothes.

How is this guy single?

Instead of sitting on the bed with me like he did in my room, he walks over to the chair near the window on the other side of the room and sits down. "So what did you want to talk about?"

I don't know why, but suddenly, it feels foolish to ask him to tell me more about his family now that I've had all these impure thoughts about his body. My mind races to come up with another excuse to be there in his bedroom this late at night, and all I can come up with is asking about the men he's hiring.

Not that I'm the least bit interested in them.

"Well, I was just wondering how it's going with finding four men you want to work with. Did the company you work for have people ready to go?" I ask, barely able to conceal my utter lack of curiosity about this topic.

For his part, Liam seems completely excited about the men and when they'll be arriving, and for the next five minutes, he talks about who they are, what their backgrounds are, why he chose them, and what seems like a million other details about these people I don't give one damn about.

Finally, he stops, but I'm focused on trying to remember what the tattoo on his lower stomach meant with its design that reminded me of some Celtic thing I saw at a store in Clearwater one time. I don't realize there are no words coming from him for a good half a minute, and when I do, I feel my face grow hot instantly.

"Oh, sorry. You were saying?"

Not my best attempt at covering up for not paying attention.

"It doesn't seem like you really want to hear about this."

I'm not sure, but I have a sense that I hear hurt somewhere beneath his words, so I quickly say, "No, no. I do. Why else would I have come here and bothered you?"

Liam smiles, and my stomach does a flippy thing at how sexy he looks right now. "I don't know. Is there any other reason you would come here to see me?"

Embarrassed, I look away and mutter, "You're very neat."

"I guess. I'm not sure I'd say very neat. Just neat."

Staring off at the curtains hiding the door out to the balcony, I ask, "Do you like your room?"

Suddenly, he doesn't seem to have much to say. "Yes."

Questions barely get answers and no detail at all, but he couldn't stop talking about all of the guys he's planning to bring onboard to work with him.

My gaze lands on the armoire that houses the TV, so I ask, "Is the TV okay?"

"Yeah."

God, why has he suddenly clammed up like he's being charged by the syllable? I've never felt this uncomfortable in my life! So much for being the owner of this house and his boss. You'd swear he's the one in charge and I work for him.

We sit silently, each second that ticks by more awkward than the last, until I turn to look at him and blurt out a thought about something I watched a few nights ago on one of the nature channels. "You know what some of my favorite shows are? Animal shows."

For a moment, he merely stares at me in what appears to be complete confusion before he finally says, "Really?"

That's all he says. Really.

So I keep going, almost as if I can't stop myself. "I saw one about a goose who had a dozen goslings. Do you know they look like geese after only a couple months? I thought they'd look like babies for longer."

He doesn't respond, so I bolt up from the bed to leave. Clearly, he doesn't want to talk to me tonight. It's okay. I shouldn't have come here anyway.

"I'm going to go."

Behind me as I take a step toward the door, he

says, "I think I watched that the other night when I couldn't get to sleep."

Suddenly, a wave of relief washes over me. Spinning around, I see him smiling. "You did? I couldn't believe how quickly those baby geese grew up to look like full grown geese. I never knew that about them."

"I didn't peg you for an animal lover," he says, still smiling at me. "Why don't you have any here?"

With a nod, I sadly admit the reality I wish wasn't true. "I'm allergic. I would love to have a dog, but I can't."

"We had a cat when I was little. A Siamese my father got for my mother before I was born," Liam says, finally giving me more than one-word answers.

Thrilled he's brought the conversation around to his family, I take a step back toward the bed and sit down. "That's so sweet. You have the greatest family, or at least it sounds like it."

Liam rolls his eyes and shakes his head. "It's not perfect. Trust me."

I want to hear all about his not perfect clan that sounds perfectly wonderful to me with its extended family and a grandmother who keeps them in line and a Siamese cat his father gave his mother. I imagine the kitten sitting in a box with a pretty pink bow tied around its neck like the perfect present.

"I bet it's more incredible than you realize," I say, trying to hide my desire to hear anything he'll tell me about them.

Unsure he's in the mood to talk much at all, I wait,

hoping to hear even one story. Tilting his head back, he looks up toward the ceiling for a few seconds and then almost as if he knows how much this means to me, Liam begins to tell me about the time he and his cousins were all nearly teenagers and got in trouble at a summertime cookout at his grandmother's.

As silly as I know it is, I hang on every word and every gesture he makes as he tells the tale, laughing when he chuckles about how his parents were furious, along with his aunts and uncles, because all the boys had stolen beer and hidden it down near the water to sneak drinks from all day. By the time they sat down to eat dinner, every one of them were drunk off their asses, each from less than a full beer.

"Of course, as the oldest boy, my father assumed I should have stopped all of this from happening. I wasn't the ringleader—that was Cade and Alex, as usual. I was nearly thirteen, which put them at ten, but the two of them were always troublemakers."

"I hope I get to meet all of these people sometime. They sound like so much fun. I wish my family had stories like that. We don't have anything but my mother and me together doing the same thing we've done for nearly all my life."

And just like that, all the happiness the two of us had been enjoying evaporates with the truth of my life. I see the change in Liam as his eyes fill with sadness, or worse, pity for me. I'm sure my mother has told him the whole ugly story of how my father couldn't hack dealing with my work to become a singer and her efforts to do everything she could to make my dream come true. It's a pathetic story of a man needing to be the center of attention and unwilling to accept he couldn't be.

Then Liam says the two words that crush me more than anything else he could utter.

"I'm sorry."

I so desperately wanted to not be pitied tonight, but with just those words, that's all I am.

"Yeah, well, you don't have to be. I need to go. Goodnight."

He doesn't get a chance to say anything, and by the time I slam his bedroom door behind me, the tears are rolling down my cheeks. The tabloids and those ridiculous social media people should get a look at me now.

No man in my bed. No good times drunk or high.

Just me alone wishing I had a different life sometimes. Is that so much to ask? I don't want to give up all I have. I just want to smile and laugh for a few minutes without having to deal with the reality of who I am and what my life has been.

I guess it is too much to ask.

CHAPTER THIRTEEN

iam

THREE TIMES TODAY, I'VE WALKED INTO A ROOM IN this house and Mia has immediately walked out. I'm not sure what's wrong, but my gut tells me it has to do with last night. I thought we had reached a new understanding between the two of us after she came to my room clearly to hear stories about my family, but obviously, I was wrong.

Her crew, as she calls them, is more like an angry gang that glares at me whenever we have the misfortune of being in a room at the same time. Probably still upset I told them the truth about their behavior the other day. Too bad. Somebody needed to.

At least one benefit of setting them straight is they appear to have found some manners. Other than the nasty staring at me, of course. Or maybe Andrea finally made it clear that having their craziness around Mia all the time isn't good for her. I saw how rattled she looked when I said she might not be able to perform.

I haven't been around here long, but I've figured out that fear of her daughter's career ending is a true motivator for Andrea. At first, I thought she was the only good person here and Mia was the tyrant, but lately, I've been rethinking that opinion.

After a long morning meeting with Javier and his people regarding the changes we need to implement here at the estate now that I know there's a stalker in my client's life, I head toward the kitchen to grab some lunch. Two days ago, the cook Cecelia made me a hell of a grilled cheese sandwich and tomato soup, so today I'm looking forward to enjoying that again, assuming the hoard of people around here haven't devoured every last ounce of it already.

Hopefully, I'll get to eat by myself since I think I saw Mia's entire crew file across the lawn toward the practice studio on the other side of the estate with the star herself and her backup dancers who've begun to come here every day now. Too bad they can't all stay there permanently.

Cecelia smiles when I walk into the kitchen, waving at me as she walks out of the pantry. "Hungry, Liam?" she asks with more enthusiasm than I expect from anyone around here. It's almost as if she's happy to see me.

"I was hoping to have another of your grilled cheese sandwiches and some tomato soup from the other day," I answer as I stop near the enormous stainless steel refrigerator.

She walks over to me and tilts her head back to smile up at me. Short and very round, she's the nicest person here by a mile. "You're in luck! I saw how much you loved my soup and squirreled some of it away for you. Let me heat it up. It won't take long, and then you can have your grilled cheese and tomato soup lunch."

"Thank you, Cecelia."

Waving me away, she turns around to start working on my food. "Now go! Get out of my kitchen and let me do my magic. Go!"

I open the refrigerator to grab a drink, and my gaze lands on that green stuff that smells like feet sitting front and center on the middle shelf. With a grimace, I look past that to the jug of iced tea and reach into grab it. Whatever that stuff Mitchell drinks wafts up to my nostrils, and I swear my eyes begin to water at the stench.

The guy clearly knows how to take care of his body, but Christ, what the hell is that shit?

After pouring myself a glass of iced tea, I head out to sit at the dining room table. Nobody else comes into this room, so it's the perfect place to avoid any of the crew who might show up.

I hear a noise and look up from my phone expecting to see Cecelia with my lunch. But it isn't her. Instead, Ainsley stands in the doorway glaring at me for the fourth time today. Goat girl sure does hate me. Why, I have no idea.

Nor do I care.

"Sitting down for a nice lunch, Liam?"

Her tone says she's planning on saying something else after that, but I really don't want to hear it because then I'm going to want to reply. So I force a smile and nod before returning my attention to the news headlines on my phone.

"You have a pretty nice gig going on here. I hope you appreciate it."

Ah. So that's where we're going with this today. The life coach who does nothing, as far as I can tell, wants to know if I appreciate how great my job here is. It might be great if I didn't have to deal with her and the rest of Mia's crew.

I ignore her, even as every cell in my body screams at me to remind her how sweet a gig she has going on here. At least I have a purpose around this house. An actual job that involves tasks I have to complete.

She merely has to get her aura into the right zone or whatever the hell she does and fill Mia's head with positivity. How goddamned hard could that be living here? This house has every luxury a person could want, the estate is kept beautiful by a legion of gardeners and landscapers so it's like living in paradise, and her entire job here is to be a cheerleader.

But Ainsley doesn't take the hint and sits down at the table with me. I feel her angry stare practically boring a hole through my face. Somebody wants to have it out with me today, although I'm not sure why.

When I finally finish reading a story about how the Bucs are probably going to be looking at rebuilding their offensive line before next season, I calmly lift my gaze and see her still staring at me. Jesus, she is an angry person. Maybe she should go find some of that Zen she claims to know so much about.

"Is there something I can help you with?"

I want to add the nickname I call her—Goat Girl —but I figure I don't need to goad her into getting even angrier than she looks right now. I'm thinking at any moment, steam will come shooting out of her ears.

"You've been a big influence on Mia lately, and I'm not sure it's a positive one," she snaps, almost spitting the words at me.

Taking a deep breath, I let it out slowly, weighing how much I want to lay into my client's life coach today. I'd love to tell her exactly how little I think of her, but Mia is close to this person and the last thing I want to do is upset the delicate balance I'm trying to achieve with her.

"I think you're confused, Ainsley. I'm the chief of security here. I work for Mia. I'm neither positive nor negative. I simply do my job and that's it."

Her eyes narrow, and she points toward the grounds outside the window. "Javier is chief of security here, so I'm wondering why you need to live here at all if you're the person who's responsible for Mia's safety off the estate."

"I'm over Javier," I say in a sharp tone to match hers. "He works under me. Is there some problem with Mia's protection that you'd like me to look into? If not, we have nothing else to discuss since you're in charge of whatever you do, and I have an actual job here."

Ainsley's green eyes grow wide and full of anger. Fuck, I should have stopped myself at the question I asked her instead of continuing on to insulting her, but I'm tired of all of Mia's crew. I have a fucking job to do. Why can't these people understand that?

"What I do for Mia is none of your business, Liam. All you need to know is I don't think you're a positive force for her, and I can't allow that to be."

She can't allow what to be? This woman and her positive force nonsense is grating on my last nerve right now.

"Aren't you in charge of making her see the positive, Ainsley? I would think that's your job to take care of. As I said before, I am neither positive nor negative. I'm simply the person in charge of her security. So why don't you go find your center or whatever the hell you do and leave me alone to eat my lunch before I have to go back to my actual job on this estate?"

By the time I finish speaking, my voice is loud enough that Cecelia pokes her head into the dining room to see what's going on. Turning to look over toward the doorway, I give her a smile that disappears the moment I return my focus to the life coach.

We stare each other down for a long moment before she closes her eyes and takes a deep breath in. I watch in confusion, hoping to God she isn't planning on staying here and meditating or whatever she does all during my lunch.

After she lets the air in her lungs out in a long exhale, she opens her eyes and smiles, but it's clearly forced. "You're right. I am in charge of helping Mia see the positives in her life. I care about Mia a great deal. She's my friend, and I'm concerned that how you see her is affecting her negatively."

Surprised by the sudden change in her demeanor, I rethink my desire to continue to fight with Ainsley and nod, still unsure what the hell her problem is but willing to at least listen now that she's not acting like she wants to attack me.

"I'm not sure what you mean. I see Mia as a client. She requires security, and that's what I'm here to provide. What I think of her or everything that surrounds her here doesn't figure into that."

As if someone turned on the nice switch on this woman, the life coach leans forward toward me and says in a low voice, "Mia is a good person. She's not spoiled or cruel, like the social media assholes say she is. She would give someone the shirt off her back if they needed it. But she's very susceptible to the people around her and how they feel about her. I sense you think she's not as terrific as she actually is."

"I don't think she isn't a good person. I'm not sure what's made you say all of this to me today, but I think Mia is a talented woman with gifts many people in this world would love to have."

Angry Ainsley returns, and she snaps, "But?"

I'm beginning to think this woman has multiple personality disorder and all her personalities are having a field day inside her today. All I want to do is eat a good lunch and return to work, but when I glance over toward the doorway and see no Cecelia with my sandwich and soup, I resign myself to the fact that I'm going to have to continue this conversation for the time being.

Even if it upsets Ainsley, which I suspect what's about to come out of my mouth next will.

"But you and the rest of her crew are a lot to deal with, which makes my job harder. Like with this stalker. Why the hell didn't any of you think to tell Andrea to give me that stalker's letter instead of handing it over to Mia? All of you are to blame for her unraveling because of that letter. She didn't have to be upset like that."

I stop for a moment, but I need to get the rest of my ideas out, so I continue. "And you know what? I think all of you thrive on the chaos that happens here, and the reason you don't like me is that I want to create order for her. If I had gotten that letter instead of her, I would have investigated where it came from and who's behind it before I even mentioned it to her in the first place. That's my job, and you all make my job much harder, which hurts Mia, even if you don't want to admit it."

Ainsley opens her mouth to snap back at me but closes it like she's rethinking whatever she planned to say. With a frown, she shakes her head.

"We don't mean to do that, but you're right. You should have gotten that letter instead of Mia. I can promise you none of us would ever want to hurt her. We love Mia. We only want her to be happy, and what happened last night made her feel anything but happy."

Feeling the tension between us ease, I smile. "We're all on the same side here. I'm not trying to change Mia or anything that happens in this house. I just want to make sure that I can protect her the best I can, and the chaos that seems to happen all the time in this place makes that much harder."

Ainsley nods, although I'm not sure she agrees with me. That's okay. I don't need her to agree with me on anything. I just need her and the rest of the crew to stop the madness so I can do my job.

With skepticism filling her expression, the life coach says, "Mia told me you said you'd lay down your life for her. Is that normal in your business?"

"Yes."

She screws her expression into a look of disgust and says, "Michael never told her that."

As much as I want to unload about how bad my predecessor was at his job, I restrain myself and simply say, "Michael wasn't good at his job."

With a smile, Ainsley says, "Michael was a tool who didn't appreciate how wonderful Mia is."

"That too."

Hoping this little conversation has ended, I look over toward the doorway and see Cecelia walking in with my lunch. Thank God. Another couple minutes of Ainsley and I'd have indigestion before I even got to enjoy a bite of my delicious meal.

She senses it's time for her to leave and stands up

from the table. "Well, I'm glad we had this talk. I guess I'll go and let you enjoy your lunch."

I force a smile, even as I'm thrilled to see her leave. "Nice talk."

As Cecelia sets the plate with my grilled cheese sandwich and chips in front of me and then sets the bowl of tomato soup next to it, she pats me on the shoulder. "You enjoy your lunch, Liam."

This time, my smile is genuine. "Thank you. This smells incredible."

"By the way, don't tell anyone I said this, but I think you're just what Mia needs here. She doesn't need any more craziness. Keep up what you're doing. It's good for her."

"Thanks, Cecelia. I'm just doing my job."

She smiles and points at the sandwich waiting for me. "Well, don't stop. I put extra cheese on there special today. I thought after that little pre-lunch meeting you could use it. Enjoy."

Finally alone, I take that first bite and love how fantastic her grilled cheese sandwiches taste. She's right about needing something more after having to deal with Ainsley and whatever the hell she was trying to tell me.

After that, what I can use is a good stiff drink, but that will have to wait until later. I've got more work to take care of today finding out who Mia's stalker is and getting the extra men I need to make sure he never gets close enough to hurt her.

CHAPTER FOURTEEN

ia

As much as last night ended up going badly, I can't deny I like how I feel when I spend time with Liam. Somehow, even though he's my bodyguard, he makes me forget about stalkers and their stupid letters, my mother and her hysteria, and everything else surrounding me.

So tonight, I want to lose myself in a marathon of the greatest seventies TV show and educate him when it comes to The Brady Bunch. I still can't believe he's never heard of it. That perfect couple in the picture definitely have one flaw, for sure.

Not five seconds after I knock on his door, he opens it wearing a pair of gray sweatpants that look different than the others I've seen him in. These have front pockets, and I swear they act like a frame around his hips and crotch so all I want to do is look there.

Does he wear these things on purpose because he wants to be a tease, or is Liam actually that straight and narrow guy who doesn't realize what he looks like in them?

Quickly, I lift my gaze to his face and smile, silently praying to God that my cheeks aren't turning as red as they feel. "It's not too late, is it? I wanted to help you become more cultured."

Liam shakes his head as a look of bewilderment settles into his chiseled features. "I'm not following. What do you mean?"

"Can I come in? It's sort of rude to keep someone standing out in the hallway like this, especially if it's the person who owns the house."

As if I reminded him of his manners, he quickly steps aside, opening the door all the way so I can walk into his room. "Sure. I'm sorry. I'm just not understanding what you meant by making me more cultured."

I notice the TV isn't on, and I wonder what he could have been doing in here. Maybe he meditates. He does seem like a very calm person. That's probably how he stays that way.

Or maybe he reads. I can definitely see Liam as a reader. He has a cerebral thing about him. He probably likes thrillers. Spy thrillers, I bet. I look around for any sign of a book, but I don't see one on his bed or on any of the other furniture.

"Were you busy doing something?" I ask as he

walks past me to stand on the other side of the room over near the glass door to the balcony.

"Not really," Liam says with a shrug. "Is something wrong? Do you need my help with something?"

Always the job with this guy. No wonder he knows nothing of great seventies sitcoms. That will change tonight.

I grab the remote off his bed and point it at the TV. "What's wrong is you know nothing of The Brady Bunch, which I think is a crime in at least ten states. I'm here to remedy that utter failure in your education."

My teasing makes him smile, and I can't help but notice how sexy he looks when he gives me a genuine smile. "And to think I was busy with math and science when I could have been binge-watching some old TV show."

Waving him over to where I sit on the edge of the bed, I say, "Some old TV show? Those subjects are nice, but the gap in your cultural education must be rectified. So that's what I'm here to do tonight."

"Aren't you too young for that show? Isn't it from the seventies?"

I look at him in shock. "Do people ask others if they're too young for the Mona Lisa? Let's get going. I think it's best to start at the beginning. We don't want you to not have the full experience."

"Oh, well, of course. I need the full experience," he says, clearly teasing me.

Undaunted, I roll my eyes. "Be sure to listen to the

theme song for the show because that tells you a lot going in, okay?"

He sits down next to me on the bed and looks at me quizzically, raising a single dark eyebrow in skepticism at my claim about The Brady Bunch theme. "So the song at the beginning of the show is important? Aren't those usually just music without lyrics?"

I click through the various screens to get to episode one and nod. "I don't know, but it's important for The Brady Bunch. The song tells you who these nine people are. Ready?"

"As much as I'll ever be," he says in a voice full of doubt and then mumbles under his breath, "Nine people. Wow."

The episode begins to play and with every important section of the theme song, I repeat the information. "So the lovely lady, she's the mother. The daughters are top to bottom Marcia, Jan, and Cindy. Cindy's the one with curls."

"Okay."

When it gets to the second verse of the song, I point at the screen and say, "So the father's last name is Brady, which makes sense since this is The Brady Bunch. His sons are from top to bottom Greg, Peter, and Bobby. A nice wholesome family."

Liam hums next to me like he's taking this all in.

The next verse begins about the lovely lady meeting the man, and I say, "So they meet, fall in love, and make one huge family that lives in the suburbs of LA."

He doesn't say anything at first, but when Alice appears in the center square, he quietly asks, "Who brought their mother to live with them? Should I assume much of the show is the hassle of having a mother-in-law around?"

God, he can be funny sometimes. I don't even think he realizes it either.

Laughing, I shake my head and freeze the picture of all nine characters in their boxes at the end of the show's intro. "That's Alice, the live-in housekeeper. She takes care of everything the kids need. There are six of them, after all."

With a smile, he nods and says, "Okay, that makes sense. Both parents work, so they need a live-in housekeeper. I think I'm getting the basics here."

I hold up my hand and shake my head as I press play to begin the episode. "No, no. It's the late sixties, early seventies, and Mike Brady is an architect. Wait until you see the house they live in. They have money. So no working for Mrs. Brady."

"Okay. She doesn't work, but they need a housekeeper who lives there with them. I guess I get it."

His disapproval of the Brady household situation comes through loud and clear, but I don't bother trying to explain that what the mom does isn't really the focal point of the show. He'll get that as we watch the episodes.

I point the remote at the TV again to increase the volume and look over at him sitting next to me.

"Ready? We're going to start from the beginning so you have a true understanding of this show."

With a smile, he says, "This feels like we should have popcorn or something."

"Maybe, but we'll get to that later. For now, you need to get this culture into your brain, Liam. Settle in and enjoy the greatest TV show of the seventies."

By the time the ending credits run on episode one, Liam is lying back on the bed with his hands behind his head like he's about to start doing crunches. The look on his face has changed from unsure to curious to disbelieving, but I remain undaunted in my quest to show him what he needs to know about The Brady Bunch.

He turns his head to look over at me and asks in a voice that tells me he's not yet seeing the true greatness of my favorite old show, "So you're telling me the parents felt bad and took their kids and the housekeeper on their honeymoon with them?"

"And the dog," I say with a giggle. "Don't forget the dog. They wouldn't leave Tiger behind."

"Of course. I guess if Alice can come along, why not bring the dog too?"

"See? Now you're getting it!" I squeal with excitement. "I'm going to grab us something to snack on and drinks. You start the next episode and I'll be back soon."

"Are we just going in order?"

I think about the episodes I like and shake my head. "No. I think we should jump to episode three. It's very cute. You enjoy, and I'll be back."

Before he can say another word, I rush out of the room, glancing back one last time to see him still lying back on the bed. Jesus, it should be illegal for a man who looks that good to wear those gray sweatpants. Seriously.

Ainsley and Mitchell are sitting in the living room and see me rush down the stairs toward the kitchen. Naturally, she follows me, curious to know what I'm up to since I must seem far more excited than usual.

As I grab a blue plastic bowl out of the cabinet for the popcorn, she comes up behind me and whispers, "What's the bowl for?"

I open and close cabinet door after cabinet door while I search for popcorn to pop. "Popcorn."

"If Mitch sees you eating that much popcorn, he's going to have you running until you drop!" she exclaims far too loudly.

Spinning around to face her, I put my finger to my lips. "Shhhh! I don't need that tonight, okay? I'm just finding some snacks while I watch some TV, so go back in the living room and keep him out of here."

"Want some company?"

I shake my head but don't explain I already have company. Ainsley doesn't like Liam, and I'm not in the mood to defend that I do right now.

"Clearly, we don't have any popcorn," I say as I close the final cabinet where food is stored. Then I remember the cook reorganized the kitchen a couple months ago and put everything like snacks in the pantry.

Ainsley follows me there as I search for what's

become the elusive popcorn I can't seem to locate. "So what are you watching all alone up there?"

I look through shelf after shelf to find no popcorn. Damn! There is a bag of chips and a half-finished bag of pretzels I'm sure Mitchell would have a fit about if he saw them, though.

Oh, well. They'll have to do.

"Why won't you answer me? You're acting very weird tonight, Mia," Ainsley says behind me as I tear open the bag of chips and dump them into the bowl.

"Just in a hurry. That's all. We can talk tomorrow, okay?" I say, turning around to give her a smile I hope will make her happy.

Armed with my big bowl of chips and half a bag of pretzels, I head back to the refrigerator out in the kitchen. Do we even have soda in the house these days? Once Mitchell said no more ever again right before the last tour, I had the cook stop buying it, but I think that assistant of my mother's sneaks some in since I've seen her drinking glasses full of something that looks like cola.

I search but find nothing except iced tea. That's okay. I like iced tea, and I'm betting Liam isn't a big soda drinker anyway. Now all I need are the glasses.

Setting the jug of iced tea, the bowl of chips, and the bag of pretzels on the countertop, I grab two glasses and tuck them under my arm. If I arrange this right, I should be able to carry all of this upstairs without dropping a thing.

"What do you need two glasses for? I thought you

were watching TV alone in your room," Ainsley says, refusing to curb her curiosity.

"We'll talk tomorrow. Okay, Ains?"

I grab everything I need to have a fantastic Brady Bunch marathon with Liam and start heading back upstairs. Ainsley follows me, as she has with every step I've taken in the past five minutes and grabs me by the shoulder just as I hit the first stair.

"Are you and Liam hanging out together up in your room?"

This time her voice is full of all the judgment I'm not interested in dealing with tonight. Or any night, for that matter.

I don't lie to her when I shake my head and hurry up the stairs without saying another word. We aren't hanging out in my room. We're in his. It's a technical difference, but a difference, nonetheless.

By the time I reach his bedroom door, I'm just about to lose my hold on the iced tea jug and the bag of pretzels, so I slam my shoulder into the door hoping he'll get the hint and answer it. Then again, he might be so engrossed in episode three of The Brady Bunch that he may not get to me in time.

"Liam! Help!" I say just loud enough for only him to hear, hopefully.

Barely a second later, the door opens and he rushes out to help me as the iced tea starts to fall to the floor. He catches it and the bag of pretzels as they slip from my hold too.

"I would have helped if I knew you were bringing

up the entire kitchen," he says with a smile as I push past him into his room.

"Close the door. I think Ainsley might be following me," I say as I sit down on the bed and set the bowl of chips and the glasses on his nightstand.

"The life coach? Why? Does she want to watch lame TV too?"

I turn to look at him knowing my expression shows how hurt I am. "Lame? You didn't like that Cindy didn't want to choose between her mom and her new dad so the school set up a special dress rehearsal for the whole family to see?"

Liam stops dead in front of the bed and looks over at me. "Jeez, you really do like this show. Okay, not lame TV. Old. Old TV. That's fair, right? I mean, this show is like fifty years old."

"The classics never go out of style, Liam. That's another sign you need more culture in your life."

He walks around the bed and takes one of the glasses from me. "What's next? Are we going to head out to some museum? I'm thinking that's where we'd find some true classics, right?"

As he pours the iced tea, I roll my eyes at his suggestion. "Stop being such a Philistine and sit down. The next episode is coming up soon. By the way, I wanted to bring up popcorn, but we don't have any in this house. We don't have any soda either. So all we get are the second tier snacks and drinks tonight. Sorry about that."

We settle in at the head of his bed, me next to the nightstand with the jug of iced tea and my glass and

Liam beside me with the half-eaten bag of pretzels in his lap, his long legs stretched out in front of him. In between us, the big blue plastic bowl full of chips sits where both of us can reach it.

"So onto the next episode?" Liam asks as he takes a handful of chips.

I grab the remote and shake my head. "I think I want to go to one of my favorites. This one is focused on Tiger, so no saying anything negative because anyone who doesn't like a family's beloved pet would be a monster."

He chews for a few seconds and says, "Well, never let it be said that I'm a monster, so let's watch another one and see what Tiger's up to."

I can't help but smile at his change in attitude. "That's the spirit."

Liam can pretend like he doesn't enjoy this, but he's having a good time. I think it's possible he just doesn't know how to enjoy himself since he's Mr. Rules and Regulations, but I'm happy to give him help with that.

CHAPTER FIFTEEN

iam

THREE HOURS OF WATCHING BRADY BUNCH episodes and I have to admit this show doesn't suck as much as I thought it did for the first half hour or so. The episode about the dog was cute, but even better was seeing how teary-eyed Mia got when they finally found him at a neighbor's house. I suspect she's watched that show at least a few times in the past, but it still makes her get emotional when everyone gets their happily ever after.

She aims the remote toward the TV and turns to face me with a determined expression. "This one is about when the family goes to Hawaii. It's actually a three-parter, so get comfortable. I think you'll like it."

I want to ask why since nothing about this show seems on the surface to have anything I've ever mentioned liking, but I don't say a word. She wants to give me more culture, so more culture is what I'll get tonight.

The show follows the formula I've noticed it always follows, even after only watching a handful of episodes, and by the time the youngest Brady boy finds some relic rumored to be cursed, I know how it's going to end. Nobody's going to end up dead, for sure. This isn't that kind of show.

"Have you ever been to Hawaii?" I ask, turning to look at Mia while I wait for her to answer.

She shakes her head. "Not yet. I'd like to go, but I've never had a show there, and when I'm off, I'm usually too beat to do much traveling."

I nod my head and then she adds, "Plus, it seems like it's not the kind of place you'd want to do alone."

Mia waves off her comment and says, "You know, cursed tiki things and all of that."

She sounds sad all of a sudden, so I say, "You could go with your life coach. I bet she'd love a nice vacation like that."

"I guess. Maybe. It just doesn't feel like a girls' trip kind of place. Doesn't Hawaii always seem more like a romantic vacation to you?"

For a moment, I think about it and then shrug. "I can't say I've thought about it at all, but I guess so. The Bradys didn't think that way, though. Then again, that mother and father bring their kids and the housekeeper on their honeymoon, so I'm not sure they understand the idea of a vacation."

Mia elbows me in the side and gives me a look of

utter disapproval. "They missed their family. You can understand that, can't you?"

"Not really. I'm not taking anyone on any honeymoon I go on. That's for sure."

Almost as if she forgets about the episode playing on the TV, she turns her body to face me and asks, "What's it like to have lots of family around you all the time? Is it as wonderful as it seems?"

My initial idea is to say hell, no, it's not wonderful at all, but suddenly I think I understand Mia's near obsession with this show. Like my stories about my family, it's something she wants but has never had.

Then it dawns on me why she keeps her entourage around her for weeks before her tour. She certainly doesn't need stylists and a personal trainer living here. The same goes for that life coach too. The only one who seems to actually do anything is the choreographer since she and Mia practice with the dancers every day now.

She wants them here so she can pretend like she has the family she's always wanted.

Maybe being part of a big family isn't perfect like she wants to believe it is, but now that I think of it, it's never been so bad either. It certainly seems a whole lot better than what she has with her mother.

I smile and answer her question as truthfully as I can. "You know, it's not bad. It can be a pain in the ass having all those people thinking they have a say in your life and what you do with it, but it's pretty great to have them around when it feels like the rest of the world wants to see the worst in you."

She sighs and nods. "I had a feeling that's exactly how it is. You're so lucky, Liam. Never forget that."

A sense of sadness hangs off her words, and I consider telling her about all the times my family got on my last nerve about something. I don't, though. Mia's built up the idea of a big loving family so much in her mind that I doubt she'd believe me anyway.

We don't say anything after that, and when the episode in Hawaii ends, I feel her head fall against my right shoulder. Turning my head, I see her fast asleep with a tiny smile on her lips and the remote still in her hand.

I move to gently slide it from her hold, but she mumbles something about Alice and the hula dance. Since I don't want to wake her, I carefully lean back against the headboard and settle in to watch parts two and three of the Bradys in Hawaii.

Mia lightly snores against my shoulder as I wonder if they brought the dog on this trip. Probably.

Nearly an hour later, she wakes up with a start and stares at me wide-eyed. "Did I fall asleep?"

Nodding, I point toward the TV and smile. "You missed their entire vacation. Do you want me to replay it for you?"

She wipes the sleep from her eyes and shakes her head. "No, it's okay. I've seen it a bunch of times. Did you like it?"

There's something so hopeful and sweet in the way she asks that, like she actually cares if I did enjoy watching the show while she slept, that I don't tell her the truth. "It had everything, right? Comedy, surfing, an ancient curse, and mystery. Who could ask for anything more?"

But she sees right through my answer and frowns. "You didn't like it."

When she hangs her head like my opinion on this show matters to her and I've crushed her with my teasing about it, I playfully nudge her shoulder to get her attention. She won't look up at me, so I nudge her again.

Still nothing.

"Hey, who cares what someone like me thinks? I've had to live with a family that size all my life. All that matters is you like it."

Finally, she nods and looks up at me. "I guess. I better go. Leave everything for the maid to clean up tomorrow."

"You don't have to go if you don't want to," I say, hating how things are ending with us for another night. "This is your house, after all. Technically, you could make me stay up all night watching The Brady Bunch."

She stands up, shaking her head. "No, I better go. Five o'clock comes early, I bet."

I quickly slide off the bed behind her and follow her to the door as a feeling that I don't want our time to end comes over me. "I liked it, Mia. I really did."

What I really liked was spending time with her, but I can't say that.

Her eyes light up, and she smiles up at me. "Well, then my work is done here."

We stand there for a moment saying nothing, and

then before I know it, she stands on her tiptoes and kisses me. It lasts for only a second, but that's all it takes to make me feel like I've been hit by a bolt of lightning.

Before I can say a word, she hurries down the hall toward her room, leaving me staring at her as she runs away and wondering why the hell I keep letting her get so close to me. I know better.

Why the hell can't I seem to follow my own rules with her?

CHAPTER SIXTEEN

iam

THANKFULLY, JONAH MADE SURE THE GUYS I requested to add to Mia's security staff are available. The last thing I want to do is have to bring four guys I don't know up to speed with this madhouse.

By lunchtime, they all arrive, so I take them out around the grounds to introduce them to what we'll be doing. As usual, Jack Newsom barely lets me get a full sentence in before he starts talking.

"Hell of a job, if you can get it, I guess," he says with a chuckle that tells me he thinks I have some special in with the owner of VIP. Jack's not terribly subtle nine times out of ten, and this isn't the tenth time.

As the five of us pass by a topiary that's either

some kind of dolphin or a mermaid, I roll my eyes and look back at the other men. "Nice to know good old Jack here never changes. As I was saying, it's Mia who we're guarding, not the myriad of other people who seem to mill about this estate twenty-four seven."

Turning around to face us, Jack walks backward with a shit-eating grin on his face and runs his hand through his light blond hair that makes him look like he should be at the beach instead of here with us. "And why would I ever change? Perfection is as nature intends it to be."

Barely twenty-five, he's got the confidence of a guy who's been on the job half his life. One of these days, he's going to learn some humility.

The one person in the group I'm closest to, Drew Larson, nudges my arm with his elbow. "These kids today. You'd swear they think they're God's gift to the world."

I can't help but laugh at his reference to a man just five years younger than him as a kid. Then again, Drew's always seemed like an old soul.

"Says the thirty year old," I joke to my friend.

"Thirty, but you try doing ten of those years with the family I had. You know what I'm talking about."

I do, and I nod my understanding. Drew's seen some shit and not only on the job. He watched his father get gunned down in his front yard when he was only seven, and then he saw his mother fall apart for the next five years. By the time he was twelve, he was in the foster care system, and I know from what

Wilder's told me about his time in there that it's nowhere you want to be.

"Yeah, I guess you get to call Jack here a kid. You still look pretty young, though," I say with a laugh as he pats his very short black hair.

"Of course I do. I'm the twenty-first century Denzel, man. You can't beat that," Drew says with a wide grin.

"Well, Denzel 2.0, what do you think of this place?" Jack asks as he turns in a full circle to admire the grounds. "I think I might have died and gone to heaven. How is it you always get the sweet assignments, Liam?"

I don't bother answering him because he doesn't want to hear that maybe if he wasn't a clown so often that Jonah would like him more. Behind us, another new guy in the group Kip Jones stays quiet as he takes in the surroundings. Practically the polar opposite of Jack, everyone calls him Kip because he refuses to answer to his given name, Trevor. He says it's a dick name, so he won't even turn his head if you say it. Someone once joked that it sounded British like Kip, and from that day on, he's been Kip. Very much an American, he says little and I'm pretty sure he hates Jack, which hopefully won't cause any problems.

"Doing okay back there?" I ask him and turn to see him nod his head and smile.

"You know, I don't ordinarily agree with Jack up there, but I have to think you did something nice in a past life to get this assignment, Liam. I'm a little confused why we're all needed, though, if she has her own security in addition to you."

Just like Kip to cut to the chase. He says little, but when he does speak, it's to the point, unlike with Jack and his constant jokes and chatter.

The last guy I've brought on, Brett Marshall, nods as Kip voices his confusion about why Mia needs more protection. The largest of the four of them, he's the one you put up front to let everyone know there won't be any fucking around on a job.

"I'm with Kip. You've said she doesn't leave the estate much, except to go on tour. But she's already got a damn legion of people protecting her, so what are we for?"

Before I can answer, Jack laughs and says, "You mean, what are we four for."

Everyone groans at his attempt at a joke, and Drew levels his gaze on me with nothing less than disgust. "I trust you. You know that. I'm just wondering why you brought Bozo here onto the team."

As Jack begins to protest being called a clown, I explain, "Because I need people I can trust on this job. It's not that Mia doesn't have security everywhere she goes, but it's been pretty fucking lax in the past. I needed to know I have a crew I can depend on, and even though Jack here is a bit much with his humor, I can rely on him like I can rely on the rest of you."

Out of the corner of my eye, I see Jack nod. I have a feeling it isn't going to be long before I pull him aside and tell him to cut the damn funny business. I don't need dissension in the ranks while I'm dealing with everything else Mia dishes out.

"What aren't you telling us?" Drew asks directly.

I've avoided getting into the craziness of Mia's entourage, but I can't sidestep that and the issue of her stalker any longer. As I start walking toward the back of the property, I struggle to find a way to explain what this job is really like. Mia can be a wonderful person to be around, but when she's not, she's hell on wheels. And those people she keeps here are a royal pain in the ass, but I don't want to come right out and say that. On top of all of those things, the security Andrea keeps around all the time doesn't seem to care as much about the client as I'd like them to.

None of these things will make any of these guys happy they took this job because I specifically asked for them, so I try to soften the reality a little while still being truthful. It's a fine line, to be sure.

"Why don't you tell us about Mia? I mean, she's gorgeous and the entire world loves her, but what's she like?" Jack asks.

I take a deep breath and stop near a group of palm trees. "She's nice. She lives here with her mother and a bunch of people just arrived earlier this month. They're her crew, or that's what she likes to call them. Hairdressers, a fitness guy, a choreographer, someone who does her makeup, and a life coach. I haven't seen the personal shopper yet, but I'm sure she'll wander in at some point."

"Wander in?" Kip asks quietly. "Sounds like this

isn't a very tight ship here, Liam. That's not your style at all."

All four of them look at me like that's exactly what each of them is thinking. "Yeah, I know, but it's been a challenge getting everyone here on the same page. People like us have different temperaments than artists and their friends, I guess. It's fine. The security at the front gate, which is the only way in unless you want to electrocute yourself, is good. Those guys are top notch. It's the others that her mother's kept around for a while who don't seem to be at our level. That's why I wanted you guys here with me."

Drew slaps me on the back, throwing his head back in laughter. "I bet you're going out of your mind here. Artists and their temperaments aren't really your style, man."

"Well, if any of them drive you crazy, the gym here is first-rate. I find that's the best place to take out my aggression."

I want to say the day after the crew arrived and that ridiculous goat noise woman who claims to be a life coach started with her nonsense, I spent extra time lifting that day. Either that or I was going to throw that woman in the pool. Repeatedly.

"Okay, so a bunch of artist types who don't follow the rules? Am I getting this straight?" Brett asks.

"Pretty much," I say, preferring not to go into it any more. He and the others will realize just what I mean soon enough. "Andrea is Mia's mother. She's also her manager. You don't have to deal with her if there are any issues, though. Everything will go through me."

"Sounds pretty straightforward. Why do I get the feeling you've left the biggest thing for last?" Drew asks, knowing me all too well.

I take a deep breath in and let it out in a rush. "I have. She's got a stalker. I just found out about him myself a couple days ago. See? That's what I mean about things being lax. You'd think someone would have mentioned that right off when I came here as her head of security, but no. Nobody said a word until she got another letter."

"Just one?" Kip asks.

"As of now. He seems to send one every time she's about to go out on tour. Well, almost every time. He didn't do it last year. I haven't found any reason why that is. The letter went through the post office, so I checked with them and they say it was mailed right in downtown Tampa. That's all I have so far, other than he misspells you're. I'm guessing a young guy, maybe local, but I don't know yet. Since Mia rarely leaves here, it's not a huge issue until she heads out on her tour. That's the main reason I wanted all of you on this job with me."

"You coordinate with the local people on security for her concerts, or are you in charge of finding enough people for that too?" Jack asks in a rare moment of seriousness.

"Her mother has always gone with locals, which I'd prefer not doing, but there's not enough time to change that for this tour," I answer, leaving out that I was brought on when the last head of security, that dickhead Michael, got fired just a little over a month before her tour starts.

All four men nod their understanding, no doubt agreeing with me that one person handling all the security details would be preferable. There's nothing I can do about it now, but having these men with me to cover as much ground as possible will hopefully be enough to keep Mia safe wherever we have to go.

"Okay, that's about it. Take the day to look around and get used to the place. We'll meet up again tomorrow when I hopefully have something more on that letter and where exactly it came from. I'll have your specific assignments then too. Until then, enjoy yourselves. Anybody have any questions?"

Jack, of course, steps forward with a big grin on his face. "Now when you say enjoy yourself, exactly what does that mean? Because I saw a pool on our little walking tour this morning, and I could do with a nice swim."

"Feel free to go anywhere you want, but if Mia and her people are there, come back later," I say with a chuckle, imagining how ugly it might get if we all descended on the pool while they were having their meditation time.

Behind me, I hear someone call my name, and I turn around to see Mia marching toward me in a red bikini and her white cover-up. I'd planned on introducing her to my crew later today, but now seems as good a time as any.

That cover-up of hers flies behind her she's

walking so fast, and she starts talking before she even reaches me. "Liam, I've been trying to find you for half an hour. Where have you been?"

"Right here. These are the additional security detail I've brought on. Let me introduce you."

I don't even get the first name out before she snaps, "Later. I'm not really interested in meeting anyone right now. Maybe you should do that when I'm not running around this entire goddamned estate looking for you. I need you to talk to my mother about these guys anyway, so go find her now."

Mia turns on her heel to hurry away, that white cover-up trailing behind her again. I'm not sure why she needed to be so rude, but I don't appreciate being made a liar in front of my people after I told them not ten minutes ago she was nice.

Without looking at them, I say, "I have to go deal with her mother. Remember, if Mia or her people are where you want to be, go somewhere else."

By the time I reach Andrea's office, I'm fuming mad. I still have no idea what the hell her daughter wanted, and the fact that she chose to be so short with me in front of the men I have to work with pisses me off more with each passing moment.

I knock on the office door and walk in as I say, "Mia said you needed to see me about the new guards? What's going on?"

Andrea gives me a blank stare and shrugs. "I have no idea. Jonah sent over all their pertinent details, and I've already got files on all of them. What else could I need? We're not going out of the country for the first leg of the tour, so I can't think of anything right now."

"Okay. Maybe we got our wires crossed. Sorry to bother you."

So what the hell was the wild goose chase about?

ALONE IN MY ROOM, I CAN HEAR THE NIGHTLY racket over on the other side of the house, but tonight, it's even louder than usual. It threatens to drown out the sound of the TV not even ten feet away from me. I wonder how the guys are handling it. I probably should have mentioned something about this when we spoke this afternoon.

Throwing my legs over the side of the bed, I head toward where their rooms are located and remember only Brett and Kip got lucky enough to be assigned a room on the first floor over in the west wing. Damn. Drew is going to want to kill me for this.

By the time I reach the top of the stairs, the noise from Mia's crew is so loud I can barely think straight. Music of all types blares from the rooms, and the two hair stylists keep running from one room to the next like some old school comedy.

Drew answers the door and shakes his head in disbelief. "Nice of you to give us a head's up about this," he yells in an attempt to be louder than his inconsiderate new neighbors.

I follow him into the bedroom and slam the door, happy to get some tiny bit of relief from the sounds filling the hallway. Jack reclines on his bed with his arms behind his head watching TV like he doesn't hear a thing. He waves to me and then goes back to whatever show he's so interested in.

"Let's go out on the balcony. It's a little better out there," Drew says.

We close the glass sliding door and I finally can hear myself think. Closing my eyes, I let the warm night air flow over me.

"Sorry I didn't tell you about them. It slipped my mind."

"I bet. Let me guess. You don't have a room over here."

I open my eyes and smile. "I complained and got a room on the other side of the house. These people are crazy. I get the whole artistic thing, but it's like they don't get that we have a job to do and it starts way before they roll out of bed right before noon. I'm sorry you have to deal with this."

"So the client gave you a different room? She must like you," Drew says, wiggling his eyebrows.

"She tolerates me, I think. I'm far too straight and narrow for her."

"You know, Liam, I've known you for a long time. You and I have worked together more than a few times, and I'm not sure you're telling me the truth here."

Confused, I shake my head. "What do you mean?"

"Well, for someone you speak so highly of, she's not very nice to you. I mean, I get not really being interested in doing the whole meet and greet thing earlier, but she's more like a bitch than anything else, from what I saw by that little performance she gave us. You deserve more respect than that. Why are you so willing to take that from a client?"

I want to tell him that I think deep down Mia's a good person. That I've seen a side to her that he hasn't gotten to see yet. I don't, though, because I'd sound too pathetic.

So I do what I always do. Stay professional.

"You know how it is, Drew. We're here for the clients. Not the other way around. You've just gotten lucky with some great assignments. I admit I haven't had to deal with a lot of clients like this one, but I'm just looking at it as a challenge. She can be a diva all she wants. At the end of the day, as long as she's safe, I don't care how she acts toward me because I know I've done my job right. That's all that matters to me."

A slow smile lights up his dark brown eyes. "That's why you get jobs like this when the rest of us don't. You're the best, man. Jonah knows it. I appreciate you thinking of me for this job, though, Liam. We work well together."

"We do. We do our jobs and people stay safe. Fuck the rest of it, right?" I say with a laugh.

He nods, smiling as he says, "Exactly. Fuck the rest of it."

"I better get back to my room. One of us has to be awake for tomorrow."

As I step out into the hallway, Mia walks out of her life coach's room. I smile, like I always do when we run into one another, but she simply turns her head and walks away.

Glancing back at Drew, I chuckle. "Divas."

He nods and chuckles before closing his door to the noise that seems to be quieting down, even just a little. Hopefully, he can get some sleep tonight, but I wouldn't count on it. I'm betting Ainsley is about to start her nightly routine of goat noises, so Drew will likely be up for a while.

CHAPTER SEVENTEEN

iam

I silently thank God for some peace and quiet as I climb the stairs to my room, thrilled to have nothing but the sound of my TV to lull me to sleep. Lost in thought about a movie I think I might want to watch, I don't hear Mia come up behind me until she speaks.

"What did you call me?" she snaps.

Turning around, I shrug. Barefoot and still in that red bikini that shows off her gorgeous body and her white cover-up, she stands with her hands on her hips looking particularly upset. She must have heard me say she was a diva. The truth hurts, I guess.

"If the shoe fits, I say wear it."

Anger flashes in her eyes. "What the hell does that mean?"

Unsure what she's referring to, I ask, "Are you saying you've never heard the saying if the shoe fits before? I can't believe that. Everyone's heard that."

I know she hates when I play around like this, but she makes it so easy.

Throwing her hands up in frustration, she says, "I know what the saying means! I'm not an idiot. I want to know why you think it's okay to call me a diva."

As I open my door, prepared to end this conversation before it goes any further, I smile at her. "I'm sorry. I meant that about my friend's goat calling neighbor over there. Good night, Mia."

Happy to avoid an argument right before bed, I shut the door behind me and lean back against it. I'm not in the mood to spar with anyone tonight, least of all her.

But a few seconds later, I feel the door being shoved against me like someone's trying to push it open. I step away from it, and Mia comes flying through the doorway, nearly tripping over her feet as she tries to keep her balance.

Standing up straight, she barks, "I wasn't done talking, Liam. Now why did you think it was okay to call me a diva?"

Sure this is the most surreal thing that's ever happened to me, I look around my room, half-expecting a hidden camera catching all of this as some joke to be revealed. Does she realize what she just asked after barging into my room to ask it?

"I can't imagine why anyone would think it would

be right to call someone who busts into another person's bedroom to berate them a diva. Go figure."

"I am not a diva!"

"Do you have another word you'd prefer to describe your behavior? And I'm not just talking about right now but before when I tried to introduce you to the new guys and you blew me and them off. You give me the word, Mia, and I'll use that one."

Her mouth drops open in shock, but I guess I shouldn't be surprised. I've rarely been this forceful with her in the past couple weeks since she was thoughtful enough to give me this room over on her side of the house.

A look of hurt fills her eyes for a second and then it disappears, replaced by more anger directed at me. "I never wanted four more guys. I didn't want any more, if anyone gave a damn to ask me."

Since she seems to have decided we're going to have this fight, I lie back on the bed and make myself comfortable. "Which I did, if you remember correctly."

"Don't act like you're doing me a favor by even talking to me. Stand up and be a man!"

Sometimes she's funny, and I don't think she even realizes it. Folding my arms behind my head, I lean back against the headboard and smile. "I can be a man lying down, you know."

That catches her off guard or confuses her. Mia stares at me, shaking her head, and finally asks, "Are you trying to be funny? Or was that something sexual and it came off stupid? Just wondering which it was so I can react appropriately."

"Go with funny because right now I couldn't be sexual if my life depended on it with the way you're acting."

I barely get the last word of my sentence out of my mouth and her eyes fly open wide full of fury. "Stop talking to me like you're my father! You are not the boss around here! I'll act the way I want and you, of all people, aren't going to stop me."

Pointing at the door, I say, "Then could you act whatever way you want outside of my room? I'm tired. It's been a long day."

Hurt fills her eyes, and she shakes her head as I watch her struggle to hold back tears. "Don't diminish my feelings just because you don't want to hear about them, Liam. I don't deserve to be called a diva, and I won't have that in my house."

"I'm sorry. I didn't mean to do that. Maybe we should just talk tomorrow."

My suggestion is met with silence, and she lowers her head to stare down at the floor. After nearly a minute, she quietly asks, "Why are you acting like this toward me? Is this how it's going to be now that you have people here you like?"

Her question and the sadness covering every word hit me squarely in the chest. I don't know why she's so unhappy, though.

"I don't dislike you, Mia. If you think that, you're wrong."

Probably heard that from her life coach. So much for coming to some meeting of the minds with Ainsley.

Still staring down at the floor, Mia refuses to look at me when she says, "Then why weren't you around like usual today? I had to go looking for you. You always get coffee early after spending time in the gym, and then you're around the house where I can find you. You weren't there. Why?"

Suddenly, I feel like I've misunderstood everything that happened today. Sitting up, I slide over to the edge of the bed and look up at her still focused on the floor.

"I had to handle things with the new guys, so I wasn't around like usual. That's why. I didn't know you needed me for anything."

"It just felt like you weren't here, and I didn't like that feeling."

"What did you need?"

Mia lets out a heavy sigh. "Nothing. I just feel better when you're around. That's it. I guess that sounds stupid, but I feel safer knowing you're nearby. When you weren't, I got anxious. It was nothing. Just forget it."

She moves toward the door, but I feel like I should stop her. We can't work together if she's not comfortable, so I need to make this right.

"You don't have to go, Mia. If you want to talk about something, we can talk. I'm not tired."

Hesitating, she looks up and gives me a tiny smile. "Are you sure?"

"Yeah. If you want to talk, we can talk."

"Do you want to talk?" she asks, and I'm surprised at how innocent she sounds.

"Sure."

Instantly, her smile disappears. "That's what people say when they're humoring you, Liam. I'm not stupid. I admit I don't get out into the world much, but there's this thing call TV here at the house. I've seen how people act when they're placating someone. I'll just go."

She moves too fast for me to stop her, so I hurry behind to follow her to her room. Just as I had before, she tries to avoid me now, but it takes very little to push the door open. Mia stands staring at me in surprise, which seems odd since she literally just did the same thing to me.

"I figured turnabout was fair play. I thought we were having a conversation," I say as I close the door behind me.

"Go back to your room. I don't want to talk anymore," she says, turning her back on me.

"Well, now I do, so let's talk. I'm sorry I wasn't around when you needed me today. Would it be a good idea for me to let you know my schedule each day so you can know where I am?"

As soon as I finish speaking, I know that came out far shittier than I wanted it to. Mia heard what I said exactly as I worried and spins around to face me with tears in her eyes.

"Does it make you happy or bring you some kind of pleasure to make me feel stupid?"

Taking a step toward her, I shake my head. "That

didn't sound like I wanted it to. I'm sorry."

"Stop saying you're sorry! You aren't sorry. You're handling me like everyone else does, and I hate it. You stopped doing that after the first few days when you set me straight on what your job is here and I respected you for that. Why are you back to handling me like I'm some fool you have to tolerate?"

"I'm not. I swear. I just don't seem to have anything to say that makes you happy. Maybe it's all these people around. Or maybe you're right and I'm acting different. I don't mean to, Mia. I liked that we were finally getting along. The past couple times we talked and I told you about my family were fun, but then you avoided me all day yesterday, and since then, things have been bad again."

I watch as she collapses onto the bed and covers her face with her hands. I don't know why she's so upset, but I'm only making it worse.

Then she begins to cry and I feel like shit.

"This is all my fault. I'm sorry, Liam. You're trying to do your job to keep me safe, and I'm a total bitch. I don't mean to be. I don't."

Taking a seat next to her on the bed, I quietly say, "You aren't a total bitch. Maybe halfway."

Mia drops her hands from her face and stares at me. "That's you trying to be funny, right?"

"Yes. I'm not known for my sense of humor, just in case you're wondering."

"And I'm known for being a diva," she says sadly, covering her face again.

I know I shouldn't try to comfort her because it

breaks all the rules I have for myself on a job, but it's almost like I can't stop myself from putting my arm around her to gently let her know everything will be all right. She melts into my embrace, resting her head against my shoulder.

"I'm sorry. I hate that I have to say that, but you deserve to hear it, Liam. I'm sorry. I shouldn't have been so rude to you in front of your guys today. You didn't do anything wrong. It's all me."

"No problem. They're used to people being rude. They're guys. We're rude all the time."

Mia lifts her head and sniffles as she wipes her eyes. "You're not. You're never rude, except when people deserve it. People being me."

Her dark eyes look all watery, like beautiful gems in a lake, and I shouldn't even notice that because she shouldn't be this close to me. But she is and I do notice, and something stirs inside me that definitely shouldn't be stirring.

"You're just being nice," I mumble, sure I should be stopping what's going to happen if one of us doesn't move in the next few seconds.

She shakes her head, and then what should never happen between a bodyguard and a client happens. Her eyes slowly close, and even though I should back away and get the hell out of her room, I don't. I watch her brush her lips against mine, instantly closing my eyes to revel in the softness of them as she kisses me. It's sweet and sexy and absolutely shouldn't be happening.

Yet I don't stop and even kiss her back, loving how

this feels while sirens and red flags go off in my head that I need to pull away right now. Or maybe a few seconds from now when it doesn't feel so good to kiss this woman.

But I don't pull away, and when she leans back, I feel the guilt rush through me. I'm her bodyguard. My job is to protect her, not make out with her. That's what the problem with that Michael asshole was. He didn't do his job because he got too close.

And now I've turned into him.

Mia slides her hand down over my chest, and my body reacts like it should because I care for her. I don't know how it happened. Maybe it was all that talking about my family. Or maybe it was the hours of The Brady Bunch we watched together. Hell, I don't know what it was, but all I know is I don't want this to end with a kiss and her hand moving toward my pants.

She leans in and kisses me again, and this time I don't stop myself. Burying my hand in her hair, I keep her mouth on mine as I slide my tongue in to tease the tip of hers. She moans softly, making my cock stiffen like it's made of steel. When her hand brushes over the front of my shorts, every cell in my body wants her so fucking badly I'm not sure I'll be able to think straight a few seconds from now.

Fuck. I need to leave this room before this mistake goes any further.

"Liam," she says in a dreamy voice. "I've wanted to kiss you for days. Was it the same for you?"

I want to answer her question with the words I know will make her happy, but I can't. This is wrong.

Every rule I've lived by in my job says I have to stop this.

Pulling away, I force a smile and stand from the bed. "It's late. I better go. Have a good night, Mia."

By the time I reach my room, I have a sinking feeling I've messed up worse than I've ever done on a job before. How the hell am I going to be a professional around her when all I can think of is how incredible her lips felt on mine and how much I want her?

CHAPTER EIGHTEEN

*M*ia

I WATCH MY BEDROOM DOOR CLOSE AND MY HEART falls to the floor. Why did he bolt like that? Didn't he want to kiss me? Why wouldn't he? He's a man. I'm a woman. It's not like I was asking him to hand over some organ of his.

It was just a kiss. A good kiss, though. A really good kiss. I know he liked it. A woman can tell that kind of thing. The way he felt under his shorts tells me he was into it as much as I was.

For ten minutes, I stare at the door and wait for him to come back. Maybe he ran down to the kitchen to get us a drink. That would be very romantic and something I bet a guy like Liam would do. Or maybe he just needed to go change into something more comfortable. That's what they always say in the movies. "Let me go change into something more comfortable." That's the cue for the other person to have the green light.

He wants to give me the green light, right?

With each passing moment that the door doesn't open and I don't hear a knock, I begin to worry he's never coming back. But why wouldn't he? I was getting all the signals, wasn't I? He cared enough to be concerned about me and not just professionally. He told me those stories about his family. We had a good time hanging out.

At least I thought we did.

After twenty minutes, I know he's not coming back. Fighting back tears, I throw on a pair of black shorts and my favorite pink flip flops, grab my wallet, and run downstairs. My mother keeps her keys to her SUV in her office, so I sneak in and grab them out of her desk.

I can't stay in this house anymore tonight. I need to get away. I need to be somewhere I don't feel stupid or unwanted.

The moment I slide in behind the wheel of the car, I feel free. Maybe I'll drive to the beach. Or maybe I'll drive to someplace like New Orleans. Or Montana. I can go wherever I want. Why shouldn't I? I have money, wheels, and the desire to be away from everything in that house.

My freedom comes to a halting stop at the security gate. Sylvester, the older guard who works nights, smiles at me, so I flash him a toothy grin and say, "Hi,

Sly! Just going out for some ice cream. Want me to bring you any back?"

For a second, he looks like he wants to let me through. He always has before. Before Liam, that is. It's clear he got to this nice old man who used to let me out whenever I wanted to leave when he sadly shakes his head and picks up the old school black phone in the guard shack.

"Just let me get clearance, miss. This will only take a second."

Clearance. This is my fucking life. I have to get permission from the man who just ran out of my bedroom when I kissed him. Anyone who thinks the life of a successful artist is all fun and games needs to see me as a cautionary example.

I rev the engine while I consider just driving right through this gate. My mother has insurance. I have insurance on the estate. Why not?

As I fantasize about gunning it and just blowing through this gate, probably scaring poor Sylvester to death, someone knocks on the driver's side window. I turn to see Liam staring at me with a look of horror on his face.

I could still bust through this gate. I want to.

Pressing the button to lower the window, I stare straight ahead as the glass disappears. He doesn't say anything at first, but I still don't turn to look at him. Check out the profile, buddy. Like it? Well, too bad. You could have had that and everything else, but you ran. Your loss.

"Planning on going somewhere, Mia?"

God, I hate the sound of his voice right now!

Still staring straight ahead at the gate blocking my path to freedom, I answer, "I don't have to tell you or anyone else in this world where I'm going or what I'm doing. I'm of age, so get this man to open this gate or I'm going to drive right through it and probably frighten poor old Sly to death. You want that on your conscience?"

In a much softer, less taunting tone, Liam says, "I wouldn't want that, no. But you know I can't let you go anywhere without protection. If you want to go out, I'll go with you."

Tears well in my eyes at his offer. He can spend time with me as my bodyguard, but as Liam, he disappears. No thanks.

Turning to look at him, I snap, "No. Not you. One of your other guys. They're here for a reason, so let's put them to work. What's the name of the one with the blond hair who smiles a lot? I liked the look of him today. Get him to come with me. Maybe I'll have a good time for once."

Hurt fills his eyes, but his voice when he answers me says he's angry. Why, I have no idea. Does he think Mr. Blond and Happy is going to want to kiss me?

"No," he answers in a clipped tone. "If you're going, it will be me who accompanies you."

"Whatever. One jailer is as good as the next, I guess."

He gets in and leans out the passenger side window to give Sylvester a smile. "It's okay. Thanks!"

As I watch the gate open, I mumble, "Thanks for making sure I can make this woman's life even worse than it was."

Liam asks where we're going, but I ignore him. If all he can be is my bodyguard, then there's no need for us to be friendly. I can be civil and ignore his presence as well as I do anyone else's.

I tear down the streets on my way to 275. Then I'll decide what to do after that. New Orleans does sound like fun. I've never been there, except for concerts, and then it's always been in and out, leaving no time to have any fun.

"Are you going to clue me in on where we're going, or do I get to sit here in surprise when we finally arrive somewhere?" Liam asks, but again, I ignore him.

Since I so rarely drive, I make a wrong turn and then another one, and fifteen minutes later, I'm sitting in downtown Tampa unsure how the hell to get to where I want to be. Frustrated and pretty sure Liam is having a good time watching me get more and more annoyed by the second, I pull over in front of some business with blue and green neon lights.

"This is where you wanted to come to? A check cashing place? Have a check you need cashing at eleven o'clock at night?" he asks with a chuckle, infuriating me even more.

"I just wanted to get out of that house. Away from everything. Away from you. And here I am, parked in front of some place I don't want to be at, just like I felt when I was at the house. Even worse, you're here to laugh at me."

Tired of feeling bad, I let my head fall onto the steering wheel. My forehead hits it so hard the horn blows, but even that can't stop me from crying. My tears come, the sounds of my sobbing filling the car.

I can't do what I want. I can't go where I want.

Worst of all, I can't have who I want.

I can have him follow me around like some overseer ready to pounce at a moment's notice to stop me from doing things I want to do, but that's it. He's too tired to kiss me, but he's not too tired to hover over me on this joyride to nowhere.

His silence tells me he was laughing at me, and it hurts more than anything else tonight. Or maybe it's just the last straw, but I fling the car door open and jump out, leaving it running. I'm unsure where I should go or what I should do, but I know one thing more than anything else at this moment.

I don't want to be what he laughs at anymore tonight.

The blue and green neon light in the window of the check cashing place distracts me, and I trip over the curb. I catch myself just before I hit the ground, my adrenaline coursing through me at the first taste of real freedom in weeks. I look down the street and wonder for the briefest moment where it will take me, but I don't care.

Anywhere is fine.

"Mia, get back here!" he yells, but I'm off running down the sidewalk in my flip flops.

Not exactly the best shoes for running, but I didn't exactly plan to be sprinting tonight. I turn around and see the car's headlights off. Of course, he turned the car off before chasing after me. That's so Liam. Always so worried about safety. My mother has insurance, dude. If someone takes her SUV while you're trying to catch me and take me back to that gorgeous prison of mine, she can just get another one.

"Mia! Stop!" he barks, but I'm half a block ahead of him and freer than I've ever felt in my life.

The warm spring night air rushes by me, cooling my already red-hot cheeks, flustered from running from a dead start. I'll have to remember to tell Mitchell how far I ran. He's always after me to do more cardio, but after hours of practice with Tiffany every day, I'm in no mood to get on that treadmill he so loves or any of the other machines in the gym he worships like gleaming metal gods.

Weaving between the smattering of people walking on the sidewalk with me, I see a woman with blond hair point but I'm gone as fast as I was there. A couple quickly steps out of the way as I barrel toward them, and as I pass, I hear the woman say my name.

I feel Liam behind me before I even hear his feet hitting the pavement. Is he wearing his shoes? Of course, he is. He's in his work clothes because this is work for him.

Who runs in shoes like those? Hell, even my flip flops are better for running than his work shoes. That's what you get for insisting on coming with me, baby. Keep up or I might slip away and then what will you tell my other jailers?

"Mia, stop this! I'm not going to tackle you to get you to come back to the car."

With a glance behind me, I see he's only a few feet away. In a second or two, he'll be able to reach out and grab me. I turn my head and a second later, I feel the hardness of his arm wrap around my body, pulling me against his chest.

"Stop this, Mia," he says in my ear.

I shake my head and try to push him away, but he won't budge. He's like a giant crushing me against him.

"Let go of me! If you don't let go, I'll scream. Those people know who I am."

"Then they'll call the cops and they'll find out I'm your bodyguard who is doing the job he's been hired for. Now stop trying to get away and come back to the car with me."

Thrashing my head left and right, I try to escape, but he tightens his hold on me even more. "You're going to crush me. Let me go! I won't run."

He doesn't loosen his hold and laughs. "Yes, you will. I learned that the hard way."

I know what he's referring to, and it isn't this moment right now. Whatever. He doesn't know or doesn't care how I feel, so he can go fuck himself.

"Let me go, Liam. You can't keep me trapped like this."

For the first time, I turn my head and focus on his expression as he stares down at me. Why does it seem like there's hurt in his eyes? What the hell could he be hurting about? I didn't do anything to him.

"I'm not trying to trap you, and I'm not trying to be your jailer, Mia."

His face is so close, and as much as I hate myself for even thinking of kissing him, that's all I want to do. "Well, you're both."

"Promise me you won't run."

"You mean like you did after you kissed me? That kind of running, Liam?"

I feel his hold loosen, finally, but I don't run. I need to hear him say something to me about what I just asked him.

But he doesn't speak. He merely hangs his head and sighs. Was kissing me so much of a burden that it requires a sigh like he's just had the weight of the world set on his shoulders?

He takes a step back from me and shakes his head. "I didn't run after you kissed me. It should have never happened, so I left before even more happened."

"Why? Why shouldn't it have happened? Don't you like me, Liam?"

I hate that my voice sounds like I'm some sad, pathetic thing. Why do I want to cry when I get frustrated? I want to be tough and strong like other people are when they're angry, but it's always the water works with me every time.

Liam simply looks sad, like he doesn't know what to say or how to make me stop asking him questions he doesn't want to answer. "It's not like that, Mia."

The tears welling in my eyes make it hard to see

him, so he looks like some watery giant standing in front of me when I ask, "Then what is it like? Tell me because I need to know. Please."

He sighs again, another sign all of this is a burden to him, but finally, he lifts his head and I see that sweetness I saw right before I kissed him tonight. "I'm your bodyguard, Mia. It's not right for me to be involved with you. That's what I mean."

I crave the feel of his skin on mine after he says that, like if I don't touch him he might disappear from in front of me, so I reach out and wrap my fingers around his pinky finger. "Why can't you protect me if you're with me? I don't understand."

His gaze moves to where my skin touches his and he winces. "Things get muddled, Mia. That's never good."

Stepping toward him, I look up into his eyes and wish my tears didn't make it so hard to see them because they're the most beautiful shade of blue I've ever seen in my life. Cool and almost icy, they somehow convey so much emotion that I can't help but stare at them whenever he's nearby.

"Would you protect me any less if you and I were together? Explain to me how caring about me makes your job harder."

Liam shakes his head. "It's not like that. It's that there needs to be a clear line between the client and me so I can do my job."

I take another step toward him, and holding his pinky, I curl our arms up between us. "What if I don't want that line between us?"

"Don't make this harder than it has to be, okay? You don't want me. You think you do because I'm always there and I protect you."

Every word that comes out of his mouth hurts, and I push away from him, releasing my hold on his pinky. "I'm not a child, Liam! Don't tell me what I want and what I don't want. I know what I want! Is it so bad for a woman to want a man who protects her? Why do you make it sound like I'm foolish for wanting that?"

"That's not what I meant."

"Then what did you mean? Tell me!"

"You only think you want me, Mia. If you met other men or got out of that house more often, you wouldn't think twice about me. I'd be that invisible thing that watches over you, not a man you want to kiss."

"Why? Because I'm Mia, so of course, I couldn't want someone like you? You think I'm that shallow, don't you? Or you think I'm some pathetic thing that never gets out of her gilded cage, so she can't know what she wants."

Liam shakes his head sadly, like he's disappointed he can't make me understand why I shouldn't want a man like him. "That's not it. I'm fucking this up, and I'm sorry for that. I didn't mean that you're shallow or pathetic. I just meant—"

Cutting him off, I hold my hand up to stop him. "I know what you meant. I'm not stupid either, Liam."

I need to get the hell away from him before I begin crying like a baby because I'm tired of him feeling sorry for me. Poor, pathetic little Mia. She has everything anyone could want, but she's not bright enough to understand she can't have the man she wants.

My feet move before the rest of my body understands it's time to run again, and I jump off the curb to dash into the street. Cars screech to a stop and horns blare, but I dodge getting hit. Liam follows me, of course. It's his job.

I don't care.

Then as if everything stops and falls silent, I hear him call my name and when I turn around, I see him collapse onto the pavement. Did a car hit him?

Frantic, I run back and find him on the ground with blood on his upper right arm. Clutching his elbow, he struggles to stand up but pushes me behind him. "Call 9-1-1. I've been shot."

I fumble with my phone to get it out of my pocket and call the cops. "Help! My bodyguard has been shot."

The dispatcher asks me questions I don't have the answers to, so I look around for a street sign. I tell her our location and she says someone's on their way.

As I hold on to him, he backs us up off the road. "Liam, they said someone's on their way. Are you hurt badly?"

He makes it to the sidewalk and behind a parked car, but then he collapses to the ground again. I stare down in horror as the wound on his right arm gushes blood, but I don't know what to do.

Dropping to the sidewalk, I kneel next to him and watch his eyes slowly close. "No! Liam, open your eyes! Open your eyes. The ambulance is coming right now. Please, Liam, open your beautiful blue eyes and say something to me."

But he doesn't move.

I stroke his forehead and gently press a kiss to it as tears roll down my cheeks. "Please say something to me, Liam. Tell me you hate me for driving down to this part of town and forcing you to run after me. Tell me what to do. Tell me you'll be okay. Tell me what I need to do because if you don't, I don't know what's going to happen."

Tell me what to do so you don't die.

LIAM AND MIA'S STORY CONCLUDES IN MYSTERIOUS!

GET YOUR COPY TODAY!

ABOUT THE AUTHOR

K.M. Scott writes contemporary romance stories of sexy, intense, and unforgettable love. A New York Times and USA Today bestselling author, she's been in love with romance since reading her first romance novel in junior high (she was a very curious girl!). Under her Gabrielle Bisset name, she write paranormal and historical romance. She lives in Pennsylvania with a herd of animals and when she's not writing can be found reading or feeding her TV addiction.

Be sure to visit K.M.'s Facebook page at **https://www.facebook.com/kmscottauthor** for all the latest on her books, along with giveaways and other goodies! And to hear all the news on K.M. Scott books first, sign up for her newsletter today and be sure to visit her website at **http://www.kmscottbooks.com**

BOOKS BY K.M. SCOTT:

Crash Into Me (Heart of Stone #1)

Fall Into Me (Heart of Stone #2)

Give In To Me (Heart of Stone #3)

Heart of Stone Volume One

Ever After (Heart of Stone #4)

A Heart of Stone Christmas (Heart of Stone #5)

Return To Me (Heart of Stone #6)

Forever With Me (Heart of Stone #7)

Heart of Stone Volume Two

Hard As Stone (Heart of Stone #8)

Set In Stone (Heart of Stone #9)

Silent As A Stone (Heart of Stone #10)

Heart of Stone Volume Three

All of Me (Heart of Stone #11)

Temptation (Club X #1)

Surrender (Club X #2)

Possession (Club X #3)

Satisfaction (Club X #4)

Acceptance (Club X #5)

Complete Club X Series Box Set

Notorious (NeXt #1)

Infamous (NeXt #2)

Ravenous (NeXt #3)

Ambitious (NeXt #4)

Flirtatious (NeXt #5)

Mysterious (NeXt #6)

If I Dream (Corrupted Love #1)

If You Fight (Corrupted Love #2)

If We Fall (Corrupted Love #3)

Corrupted Love Trilogy Box Set

Crave (Addicted To You #1)

Adore (Addicted To You #2)

Shatter (Addicted To You #3)

Claim (Addicted To You #4)

Addicted To You Series Box Set

In The Darkness (Project Artemis #1)

After The Storm (Project Artemis #2)

Behind The Scenes (Project Artemis #3)

Project Artemis Box Set

Hard Work (Finding The One #1)

Big Love (Finding The One #2)

Sweet Things (Dirty Boss #1)

Private Secretary (Dirty Boss #2)

Play Date (Dirty Boss #3)

Dirty Boss Volume One

K.M.'S BOOKS ARE IN AUDIOBOOK TOO!

BOOKS BY K.M. SCOTT WRITING AS GABRIELLE BISSET:

Vampire Dreams Revamped (A Sons of Navarus Prequel)

Blood Avenged (Sons of Navarus #1)

Blood Betrayed (Sons of Navarus #2)

Longing (A Sons of Navarus Short Story)

Blood Spirit (Sons of Navarus #3)

The Deepest Cut (A Sons of Navarus Short Story)

Blood Prophecy (Sons of Navarus #4)

Blood Craving (Sons of Navarus #5)

Blood Eclipse (Sons of Navarus #6)

Blood Ascendant (Sons of Navarus #7)

The Sons of Navarus Box Set #1

The Sons of Navarus Box Set #2

Stolen Destiny (Destined Ones Duet #1)

Destiny Redeemed (Destined Ones Duet #2)

Love's Master

Masquerade

The Victorian Erotic Romance Trilogy